To H

I hope you enjoy this
work of theological horror
set in the Southern U.S.
*Michael Pitts*
May 10, 2019

# OBEDIENCE
## A NOVEL

# OBEDIENCE
## A NOVEL

## MICHAEL POTTS

WordCrafts

Published by WordCrafts Press
Tullahoma, TN 37388
www.wordcrafts.net

*"Ye are of your father the devil, and the lusts of your father ye will do. He was a murderer from the beginning, and abode not in the truth, because there is no truth in him. When he speaketh a lie, he speaketh of his own: for he is a liar, and the father of it."*

John 8:44
King James Version

*"For such are false apostles, deceitful workers, transforming themselves into the apostles of Christ. And no marvel; for Satan himself is transformed into an angel of light."*

II Corinthians 11:13-14
King James Version

AD MAIOREM DEI GLORIAM

# CONTENTS

# CHAPTER 1

All seems normal - an idyllic painting, the sky dyed with pastels of blue and white, the ground carpeted with dark green fescue and bluegrass. A clapboard farmhouse rests on top of a hill. Sugar maples, oaks and Eastern Red cedars provide welcome shade from the heat of a Tennessee summer sun. All seems like a pleasant dream that recalls images of children running barefoot through the grass, an era before tweeting and texting and the triumph of technology over all. Alas, appearances lie, whispering twisted fantasies in the darkest part of the night.

Looking in from Allenville Road, to the right and behind the house rests a red barn. It looks bright and new and might fool someone into picturing a peaceful pastoral life on the farm if it weren't the color of fresh blood. Some locals close their eyes when passing by the barn, lest the odd angles at the corners make them faint. Others say the barn is obscene and draws evil out of people, leaving behind soulless shells and wrecked lives. The only thing that saves the property's reputation is the man who lives there with his wife and daughter: Sheldon Sprigg, minister of the Hare's Corner Church of God Incarnate.

Michael Potts

Today seems like any lazy summer day in the Appalachian foothills of Tennessee. Two girls, both sweet sixteen, sit on the side of the porch, their legs hanging off the edge as they sip glasses of iced tea. Susie Cottrell, the best friend of Sheldon's daughter Ginny, is busy indulging a disease of today's youth - texting on her iPhone. If odd angles were friendships, Ginny and Susie would fit right in. Ginny is rural Southern and religious to the core. She wears jeans instead of shorts, and her auburn hair hangs over a red tee shirt with the logo on the front, "Shady Grove Christian Youth Camp." Susie is what Bud Ryan down the road calls "an illegal immigrant from the north," a native of Brooklyn with an accent to match. She is blond and wears shorts that test the limits of even moderate Methodists. She also dons a designer shirt, the neckline of which is devoted to revealing her well-invested assets, to the great appreciation of her many boyfriends.

Ginny turns toward Susie, a smirk on her face that is the harbinger of a scolding. "Don't you ever stay off that iPhone?" she asks. "I swear, that thing will replace your hand one day. Talk to me like, well, like friends used to talk."

Susie types for a few seconds and puts the cell in her purse. "You're so old-fashioned," she says. "You know I can talk and text at the same time."

Ginny laughs. "Yeah, like you can drive and text?"

Susie sticks her head up in faux offense. "I only did that once. I had insurance."

*Yes you did, silly girl*, Ginny thinks. *You may be my best friend, but you sure can be stupid. Like totaling your car while texting a member of the Morhollow High School football team - another boyfriend. You got lucky that day,*

2

*proving to all that you could survive such a bad wreck without getting a scratch. I thanked God for the miracle, and you thanked State Farm Insurance.*

Ginny senses that Susie feels out of place in the rural South. Despite more diversity among students, teenagers still have that cliquish tendency that excludes those who don't quite fit in. Susie compensates by having friends from every social group, including jocks, nerds, and those whom Ginny's mama, Elma, labels "unsavory people."

Ginny rolls her eyes and laughs. "You're lucky you have your life. I saw that pic of your car in the paper."

Susie sighs and entwines her hands under her chin. She looks up with an air of confidence. "I'm obviously alive now. Don't worry, I won't text - not even with my boyfriends - when I drive. Satisfied?"

Ginny laughs. "You and your boyfriends. How many do you have?"

Susie counts one at a time with her fingers. "Let's see - there's George, and Billy, and Michael, and..."

Ginny smirks and interrupts her. "All right, don't rub it in. You can have them all. I'm in no hurry to get a boyfriend."

"Umm, really?" Susie says.

There is a moment of silence. *She wants to set me up on a date*, Ginny thinks. Before Ginny can come up with a sufficiently sarcastic reply. Susie holds her arms against her chest and shivers.

"It's cold out here, like, just now," she says.

Ginny feels the chill herself. "It sure is cold all of a sudden. Where did the upper eighties go?" Ginny asks. "Shall we call Channel 4 and file a complaint with the meteorologist?"

Susie laughs. "Your place is always cold. Ninety

degrees everywhere else, and here I feel like I'm at the North Pole."

Ginny smiles and shakes her head. "O come on, it's not that bad. The breeze is a bit cool right now, but most of the time it's nice in the summer. You're from the north - you ought to feel hotter."

"If you put it that way," Susie says, "I'll take 'hotter' as a compliment."

Ginny takes a deep breath and says, "Has anyone told you that vanity is a sin?"

Susie fiddles with her purse and mutters, "No, you're the first," and pulls out her iPhone. She perks up and says, "Hey let's get away from here and take some pics. I need a new one of you - your pic online must be three years old. You look like you're in diapers."

Ginny laughs. "You're right. I do look like a puny little kid in that pic. I guess it's about time to take another. But I can't go far. Mama's gonna want me back before dinner."

Susie rolls her eyes. "You mean lunch."

Ginny laughs and puts her hand on Susie's shoulder. "I mean *dinner*. That's what us poor, dumb, country folks in Tennessee call the noon meal. We call the late meal *supper*."

"Whatever," Susie says. She rubs her chin with her hand, looking like a mischievous muse.

"Hey," she says. "I know. Lean against the back of your barn. That red will make you stand out for sure."

Ginny wraps her arms around her chest and shudders. There are times she wonders whether Susie is of sound mind, and this is one of them. "That barn creeps me out. It's like it never changes. Weird. Bad things happened there."

Susie stands, stretches, and says, "Now *you're* the

one who's cold. But I get what you're saying. The barn creeps me out sometimes, too. I don't know what you mean by 'bad things happening,' but the barn is just a building. Besides, imagine how cool this pic will be - Ginny stands by a haunted barn - *and lives!* Your nerdy friends will love you - especially Paul, if you know what I mean."

Ginny blushes, giggles, and covers her face. She's always liked Paul from the moment she met him in chemistry class, and now that he's her lab partner, her heart flips into a faster tempo the moment she stands beside him. Still, she stays coy with Susie.

"How do you know I like him?" she asks.

Susie smiles and says, "Are you kidding? The way you look at him when he passes by in the hall? I swear, he gives you the eye, too."

Ginny uncovers her face and walks toward the barn, her lips holding the hint of a smile. The chance to impress Paul is the clincher. "Okay, you've convinced me. Let's take some pics. To heck with that old barn."

Susie's mouth hangs open. "Wowza. You said 'heck.' Radical, girl, for you. Pretty soon you'll be saying 'hell.' Just don't let your father hear it."

Ginny laughs, but inside is a tremor of terror of Daddy's temper that has turned white hot the last six months. "I hope not!" she says. "Daddy would kill me."

"Literally?"

"Literally."

Ginny doesn't mean that. Or does she? Daddy's changed from an ordinary prude to super-prude, raising the subject of hell every day. He's been telling Ginny that she's rebellious and sinful and will burn in hell when she dies. Worse, he has tried to control her life, limiting her time hanging out with Susie, calling Susie a Papist slut. Ginny doesn't dare challenge him when he's in these moods, but Mama tells her privately that Daddy's being too hard. So far that has been the limit of Mama's protests other than the lame phrase, 'Now, Dear...' As if that will do any good. Daddy is paranoid, claiming that Susie, who is Roman Catholic, though not a very religious one, 'is trying to make you worship Mary and die an idolater.'

A week ago Daddy was chopping wood. Ginny overhead him saying, just as he split a log in half, 'This is what happens to God's rebellious children.' Ginny hopes that all Daddy means is that the terribly wicked, like murderers and child molesters, should lose their heads. Still, her spine retains a hint of the chill she felt then.

Ginny and Susie walk toward the barn. The air is still, the former breeze having passed away. Ginny descends into the border of dried red clay, devoid of life, that surrounds the barn and poses. Susie snaps a photo with her iPhone, checks it out, and gives Ginny a thumbs-up.

"Lookin' good, girl. Paul will eat you up when he sees this pic."

"Stop that!" Ginny says, her laughter reverberating off the blood-colored wall behind her, as if the building were incapable of absorbing mirth. Ginny hardly notices, and Susie snaps another photo, looks it over and nods, smiling.

"Third time's the charm," Susie says, and she takes a final photo. She lifts the phone to her eyes, shrieks, and slams her hands over her eyes. The phone slips out of her hands and falls on the ground. Ginny rushes to Susie, who is now kneeling on the grass like a penitent sinner before an altar, her body trembling. Ginny wraps her arms around Susie's shoulder.

"What's wrong? You look like you've seen the devil himself."

Susie stares at Ginny with saucer-eyes, takes some deep breaths, and says, "That is the freakiest pic I've ever seen. I'm either stuck in a dream or I'm nuts. I guess my dad moving out to live with that slut fried my brain."

Ginny tries to lighten the mood, remembering Susie's grief when her dad, Dan Cottrell, ran off with a blond floozy who worked in his office complex. "You seem solid to me," Ginny says. "Do I seem solid to you?"

Susie manages a laugh, and Ginny lifts the iPhone from its resting place. She turns to the screen and retrieves the last photo.

Ginny's hands freeze. Her eyes lock on the pic. Her head spins. Ginny's image and the barn sway back and forth. A shadowy shape - someone hanging from a rope - is burned into the blood-red wall. Ginny can't move, the iPhone suspended in front of her face like a permanent prop. Susie's voice startles her, and she snaps into attention. "Okay," Susie says, "I hate Chicken Little, and the sky's still here, so let's figure this out."

They both lock their eyes on the barn wall. Nothing unusual is there. Susie takes the iPhone, scans the pic, and Ginny smiles at her fierce expression. Susie - brash, brave, Brooklyn - a rare find of a friend.

"Do you have any idea who that dude on the rope is?" Susie asks.

*Right,* Ginny thinks. *As if we're going to figure this out like two TV detectives. Maybe if we found a skull in the ground, but a supernatural shadow photo? Give me a break.*

She closes her eyes and keeps them closed as she shifts back to the iPhone. She opens them again and takes a second look at the photo. There's something familiar about the shape of the face.

*Oh, God. No, it can't be possible.*

She takes the iPhone from Susie and takes a closer look at the photo until it is at the inner range of her eyes' focus. She tries to think of the right words, but what she sees is beyond language. She turns to Susie, and words limp from her mouth. "What in the name of... I mean... shadows do funny things, right?"

"I dunno," Susie says. "Looks real to me."

Ginny clutches her arms to her chest and visibly shivers. She shakes her head repeatedly in a gesture of perpetual denial. Susie grasps Ginny's shoulders and looks her straight in the eye. "What's up? What is it you know that I don't? Tell me who's behind the shadow."

Ginny reflects on the shape of the shadowy figure, focusing on the face. The shape reminds her of an old photograph, and she shudders, considering that similarity can be coincidence, that shadows aren't as sharp as reflections, that the story Daddy told her doesn't match what she sees. She turns to Susie and speaks slowly in a low voice.

"Mostly I've heard rumors. My granddaddy died in the barn before I was born. For some reason Daddy's never hung, I mean, put up photos of his relatives, but snooping around one day I found Granddaddy's one day in an old album in a drawer in Mama and Daddy's bedroom. Granddaddy was a load of skin and bones and not much else. He died before I was born. Daddy said the floor of an overstuffed hayloft collapsed, and the bales crushed and buried Granddaddy. The shape of the face in this pic reminds me of him in that photo."

"No way!" Susie says. "The way that barn is preserved - creep factor one of many - I don't buy into that story. Sorry if I sounded disrespectful, you know, calling the man hanging 'dude.' I didn't know he was your relative."

Ginny gives Susie a hug and whispers ominously, "Don't be disrespectful again if you know what's good for you, girl?"

Susie laughs nervously. "What if this is a nightmare and you're planning..."

"...to do what?" Ginny asks. "Give me a break. I'm not Ginny the Godfather."

Susie points to the photo. "Are you totally sure this is your grandpa? I mean, it might be, but the photo's so blurred that I can't even tell whether a man or woman is hanging."

Ginny sighs. "I 'spose. The product of an imagination taxed by too much iced tea. There's no way to check out who's in that photo."

"Who or what?" Susie says.

Ginny punches Susie in the arm. "Don't freak me out any more than I am."

"I have to try," Susie says, and she springs to her feet, pulling Ginny up. She whispers in that tone Ginny knows means mischief. "Maybe there is a way to find out more. You know, get inside the barn and look around."

Ginny considers for a moment whether Susie is off her rocker in an alternative world called "Stupid." She shakes her head in a vigorous gesture of "Hell, no," huffs, turns toward the house, and starts to walk. No need to move from that particular frying pan into the fire.

"Daddy always said people from New York are crazy," Ginny says. "Now I know it's true. A minute ago you were so scared you could barely move. Now you want to check it out? No way."

Ginny picks up her pace and gets out of breath. For one time in her life she regrets she's not a runner like Susie, but it's so much easier sitting and lying down rather than jogging four miles a day. That's what cars are for. Susie runs toward Ginny and takes her by the arm, pulling her around.

"You can always catch up to me," Ginny says. "That's God's way of getting me back for being a couch potato. But you better make this good, or I'm going back to the house."

Susie stands tall and holds up her head like a proud statue. "Are you still scared?" she asks. "It was being so surprised that made me look scared. I was never really afraid."

Ginny doubles over in laughter. "Never really afraid! You lie worse than Daddy after a fishing trip. You think I couldn't feel your heart pounding."

"Must have been your own heart," Susie says. "If mine was fast, it was from excitement; the chance of finding something new. Where I grew up, a creepy building was nothing. People talk about trolls on the Internet - I'm used to trolls on the street - and they're meaner than those online. Come on; this will be the coolest thing I've done since we moved down here. Think about it. What if we find something that will tell you what is behind that shadow man? I know you're curious. This will eat you inside until you find out."

"How do you know we'll find anything helpful in the barn?" Ginny asks. "'It's 'just a building,' isn't it?"

"Don't mock me," Susie says. "The barn's our best chance. I doubt you'll find out any other way."

Ginny shakes her head and says, "Daddy would kill me with slow torture. He's been acting weird anyway - yelling at me over little things, telling me he's afraid I'll go to hell."

Susie laughs. "Why would he think that? You're an old-fashioned goody-goody two-shoes. You're the subject of the Adam Ant song. You might know it since it was a hit *before* we were born."

"Don't get smart, Susie. I know the song. Daddy heard it on a TV special one time, and he almost threw a vase at the screen."

Ginny is quiet a moment and turns her head to the side, motioning Susie to an area by the fence line. Then she says, "He's upset about what he thinks are sins. Like when I told Mrs. Hackney down the road that she has the prettiest baby I've ever seen. Daddy was angry with me and later said I lied and would go to hell if I didn't repent."

Susie growls and grits her teeth. "That's such a dumb thing to say. All babies are beautiful. Why would your father get so upset with you over that?"

Ginny giggles "Because Mrs. Hackney's baby is like the ugliest baby ever."

Susie laughs and asks, "What makes the baby so ugly?"

Ginny struggles to control herself, "Because she looks like a cross between a bulldog, a hog, and a possum."

The girls double up in laughter. Ginny says through

her giggles, "My Uncle Don would have said the baby was *butt-ugly*, but the real problem is the baby's face looks like a butt."

"Does her butt look like a face?" Susie asks, and the girls fall to the ground, rolling over and holding their stomachs. Before they can die laughing, they catch their breaths, and Ginny says, "I needed that so bad."

Susie turns serious. "Shrug off what's going on with your father. He may come around," Susie says.

"Yeah," Ginny says. "Mama says he's *going through a stage.*"

"Right," Susie says. "Like my dad's going through a stage. I don't get it. As weird as things have been today, I wonder if your father's problem is related to what happened in that barn. It's tough to see a parent die..." Susie stifles a sob. "...or leave.

"We should sneak into the barn now. Your father won't be back till later, right? It's an old barn; nothing more. Maybe it looks so good because people made paint better back then, or your great-great grandpa had a secret paint recipe based on moonshine. That weird pic only made us dizzy because of those screwy angles. We won't look up at those corners when we're inside. If there's a ghost, it won't hurt us either. All the ghost shows say that they're more like harmless whiffs of air."

"I suppose so," Ginny says, regarding her friend.

There are times Ginny feels sorry for Susie, especially after her dad left her mom. *The fool. Monica is a beautiful woman and doesn't deserve a faithless man.* Ginny wants to follow Susie into the barn to humor her, to give her a chance to have fun, to forget about losing her dad. Ginny has to admit she's curious, too.

*Susie suffers from fool-osity,* Ginny believes, *foolish*

*curiosity, a condition that's contagious. Susie doesn't care if something scares her half to death; she'll go right back to what scares her. If I don't go with her into the barn, Susie will go by herself, huffing and puffing the whole time about how she's learned twenty ways to defend herself with deadly force using her bare hands. But one last time I'll try to discourage Susie.* Ginny says, "I don't like this at all."

Ginny is not surprised when Susie says conspiratorially, "Who knows? Maybe your dad's hiding something valuable in there."

Ginny recalls the time she and Susie were sneaking around an abandoned house. *Lordy mercy if Daddy had found out.* Susie skulked up some decrepit stairs and discovered an opening in the wall covered by a board. She managed to pull down the board and worm her way inside a crawl space where she found a box of jewelry. To her credit, she didn't take the entire box, but she took two ancient, gaudy necklaces. Ginny scolded her, but Susie said, "Do you really believe the owners will ever come back? You know they've forgotten about that box by now."

Ginny cannot allow that to happen again. She says, raising her voice, "We didn't know who owned that abandoned house. We know who owns this barn; and Daddy won't forget if he finds something missing from that barn. Neither you nor I are going to steal anything in the barn. I don't care if there's anything valuable."

"Fine, fine, I won't take anything. But you'll at least get inside the barn?" Susie asks.

"I don't know if we can get the key to the padlock," Ginny says. "Daddy has to visit people from church all day and won't be back before supper. I have no idea where he keeps the key. If he took it with him, we'll never get in."

Susie laughs and says, "We won't need a key. It's just a padlock on a chain, right? Well, I picked up a few tricks in Brooklyn. Tell your mom we're going for a walk. We'll sneak around the other side of the barn to the front so she won't see us."

"Unless she goes out the back door to pull laundry off the line," Ginny says. "But she just put it up, and it won't dry for a couple hours."

"Great!" Susie says.

Ginny sighs. "Fine. This freaks me out, but I'm going with you. If this scares me to death, I'll haunt you forever. Let's grab some flashlights."

Ginny and Susie walk to the back screen door and into the house. They pass through the kitchen where Elma, Sheldon's wife, is cutting slabs of ham. "Hello, girls," she says. "What mischief are you up to today?"

"Oh, just goofing off and talking," Ginny says.

"Susie, your mom called. She wants you home by 4:30 today to help her fix supper."

Susie whispers in Ginny's ear. "She should have said *dinner.*" Ginny punches her in the arm.

"We'll be going outside in a few minutes," Ginny says, and Susie chimes in, "We're planning a walk in the woods."

"Be careful out there," Elma says. "Make sure you're both back before 4:30. Ginny, I'll need your help fixing supper, too."

"Yes, ma'am," Ginny says. She doesn't mind helping Mama, who stayed nice when Daddy turned mean. Daddy yells at Mama way too much since he changed for the worse, and Ginny constantly guards her temper lest she should say something she will regret.

Ginny and Susie step into the living room. Ginny

opens a door in a cabinet and retrieves two flashlights. She gives one to Susie.

"I think there's an electric light inside the barn," Ginny says. "But it may not work. Better to be safe."

"Agreed, O wise woman of Tennessee," Susie says.

"I'm glad you agree, smart-as..., I mean, smart-aleck girl from New York."

Susie giggles. "You almost said, *ass*."

Ginny raises her eyebrow. "How about me kicking yours?" Ginny says.

"Good one," Susie says. "I'll be meek as a mouse from now on."

"For the next minute or two, at least" Ginny says.

She puts up with Susie's smart mouth. Daddy always says that people from the north are smart-alecks who think they're better than anybody else, but Ginny sees enough people in Tennessee who are the same way that she's decided that smart-mouthedness is a universal trait. She doesn't mind Susie's - most of the time.

Ginny and Susie exit through the back door and meander toward the barn. Ginny keeps an eye on the house as they skirt along the front of the barn until they reach the chain with the padlock. Susie pulls a tool out of her pocket and quickly picks the lock and pulls it off.

"I'm impressed," Ginny says. "Is that how you filled your jewelry box?"

Susie sticks out her tongue. Ginny laughs and unwraps the chain, lowering it slowly to the ground to minimize noise. She cracks the door, and Susie pushes her way in front of Ginny to step inside first.

# CHAPTER 2

Susie steps inside the barn, followed by Ginny. *Susie always has to be the tough girl,* Ginny thinks. A sliver of sun illuminates the light switch and Ginny flicks it, but there is no effect. "No surprise there," she says. She flicks the switch back to the off position and looks around. What little sun gets in forms a shaft of light that illuminates floating dust specks. They switch on their flashlights and walk side by side on the dirt floor. Their beams reveal a hole about three feet wide in the back.

"Hey, dig that hole," Susie says, and giggles.

Ginny groans. "That is a painful pun," Ginny says. "It will burn in pun hell."

"Shit," Susie says, and Ginny bites her lip. "Even puns are damned in Tennessee. Poor puns, melting in hell."

Ginny looks at Susie and smirks. She pauses, then says, "Let's shine our lights down the hole. Maybe there's something interesting there."

"*Interesting,*" Susie says. "You sound like Paul. You two are perfect for each other."

Ginny ignores Susie, and they shine their lights

into the hole, which remains as black as a lightless cave. Ginny shivers. The blackness reminds her of the palpable darkness she experienced in Mammoth Cave. She had visited the caverns during a Science Club field trip, and the cave guide extinguished the lights to show just how dark the absence of light could be. It felt like the loss of hope. Until now she had never peered into such darkness.

Susie stares at the hole and says, "Geez, it's like there's no light coming out of our flashlights."

Ginny turns and checks the end of her flashlight, then Susie's. "The lights are still shining - bright LEDs. You're right. Their light doesn't make a dent in this dark. That's really weird."

"Creepy as hell," Susie says. "How deep do you think it is? It looks like a bottomless pit."

"Umm," Ginny says. "There are sinkholes around here where water ate away the limestone. They usually lead to underground caves, though most of those are full of water." She sniffs and makes a face. "Ugh, what's that smell?"

Susie kneels down and sniffs over the hole. She pulls back, holding her hand over her mouth and nose. "Stinks like burning sulfur. My dad, when he was around, read all the popular science rags and loved to show me things. He burned some sulfur outside one day. It made a cool blue flame, but it stunk like hell."

"That's what hell is, fire and brimstone," Ginny says. "But I doubt this smell has anything to do with hell. There's some sulfur water wells around here. I bet the stink is underground sulfur water."

"How can people drink that shit?" Susie asks, but before Ginny can answer, her head clouds over as if a spider's web were cloaking her mind. She grabs her head and says, "Ugh, I'm feeling funny."

Susie stumbles and snatches a support beam. "Me, too. Getting dizzy. Bet that water in the hole has more than sulfur in it. Christ, we're being poisoned."

There is a ringing in Ginny's ears like an alarm. She recalls the last time she heard that alarm, when she was picking blackberries from a grove in the field. She jumped back just in time to miss a rattlesnake's lunge, the flat head stopping about an inch from her leg as the mouth snapped shut. The alarm grows louder, to the point that if her mind were ears, she would go deaf.

"We need to leave the barn. Now," Ginny says. Ginny and Susie stagger toward the door, but they stumble and fall, striking the front wall. They slide into a seated position, gulping air and staring at the barn's interior. Susie breaks the silence. "Oh, shit. I was so dizzy. Like I was drunk. I know how that feels."

"I don't know how *drunk* feels," Ginny says. "I know I can't stand up. I'm not sure this is poison gas. Something else in this barn is causing this. Maybe something alive?"

"You're freaking me out, girl," Susie says. "I hope it's not something dead that can still slither."

"Now you're freaking *me* out," Ginny says. "Let's try to slide toward the door."

They scoot closer to the door, but before they go far the doors swing open and a man, pale and skeletal, trudges inside. He shuts the doors, moves to a corner Ginny thought was empty when she saw it earlier, and retrieves two long planks, which he sets against the doors to prop them shut. Ginny's body jerks in surprise, and she tries to speak. Finally, she croaks, "Granddaddy? But you're...dead."

"Oh shit, I see him, too," Susie says. The girls tremble, but the man behaves as if Ginny and Susie are not present. He moves to a dusty shelf and retrieves a rope that wasn't there moments before. He throws it over a beam near the ceiling. It catches, and he pulls it taut. Then he walks to an empty corner and returns with a platform ladder, which he sets on the floor under the rope. He climbs the ladder, ties one end of the rope to the beam with a hard knot. He takes the other end and ties it with a hangman's knot, forming a noose.

Ginny's head tells her she can do nothing, that this deed happened long ago. Not even her Father in Heaven can reverse time, regardless of what Ginny's illogical father on earth might think. Yet her heart wants to save this man, her granddaddy, from suicide and eternal damnation. Although she knew Katy, her classmate, who killed herself with pills last year, and did not want her to go to hell, Ginny could not shake her daddy's logic on suicide. *How can you repent of a sin if you don't have a chance to repent? Since God does not forgive unrepented sin, ergo...* Lately she wonders, though, whether people are not in their right minds when they kill themselves. *Would God damn someone who doesn't know what he's doing?* She doesn't know for sure. But Granddaddy seems to know exactly what he's doing.

Ginny whimpers at the thought of her granddaddy suffering in hell, so she gathers her voice and shouts, "No, Granddaddy! Not this!"

Her granddaddy ignores her. Ginny stands up, her

body feeling like a lead lump, and forces herself forward. She reaches Granddaddy who has now placed the noose over his neck. She extends her hands to stop him, but they pass through Granddaddy's body as if no one were there. Granddaddy steps off the ladder and hangs, but his neck does not break. His body twitches, writhing without purpose like a newly beheaded snake.

Ginny sobs, desperately grabbing at the empty space of the vision of Granddaddy's body. The twitching stops. The man's eyes bulge, and the tongue protrudes. His face turns purple, then black, and Ginny twists away, holding her stomach. She crawls to the hole in the floor and vomits into it. She inhales the noxious gas and backs away, barely able to move but manages to crawl back to Susie.

Immediately the barn door opens, and three goats stride inside, moving straight toward Ginny. She tries to shift out of the way, but her legs won't budge. She extends her arms to block the coming blow. The goats reach her, their hoofs trampling the floor. Susie screams and tries to cover Ginny, but the goats pass through them as if moving through empty space, hoofs insubstantial as their bodies.

The goats climb Ginny's granddaddy's body as if it were a tree, their back hooves latching onto his trunk like the boot of an old fashioned telephone line repairman onto a pole. With their front hooves they gouge out Granddaddy's eyes, leaving behind jelly-like remains of eyeballs, green-blue and mixed with clotted red blood. The goats climb down, looking like grotesque humans with goat heads. They reach the bottom and stand on their hind legs, their front legs dancing, leaving shadows on the floor like some obscene medieval Satanic Sabbat. Then they rumble outside, and the doors slowly shut on their own.

Ginny screams until her voice is hoarse, but no one arrives to help. Susie sits still, saying nothing. Nothing happens for a few minutes. Susie turns to Ginny and asks in a trembling voice, "Is it over?"

"I think so," Ginny says. "I'm praying hard that it is. Let's try to walk."

They are able to get up, but the girls feel faint and heavy, as if pinned to the earth like a magnet on steel, and they sink back to the barn floor. The doors swing open.

"Oh no, not again," Susie says, and she stretches out her hand out to reach Ginny's.

A boy of around twelve steps inside, looks up, and screams.

Ginny shouts, "Daddy!"

All the figures disappear. Ginny and Susan sit still. Ginny is afraid that if she stirs something else will awaken. She picks up her flashlight and shines it toward the doors, which are slightly cracked, the way she and Susie had left them. She believes the vision is over, and even if she had doubts, staying in the barn is a loser. If Daddy caught them inside...

*Thank God he's out visiting church members today.*

Ginny struggles to stand, but falls down, this time from exhaustion rather than from some supernatural force pinning her to the floor. She feels as drained as a squeezed sponge. Susie stands up and takes Ginny by the arm. She starts pulling Ginny toward the door, but Ginny straightens her feet and says, "I can run."

They reach the door and slip through the crack.

They begin running toward the house. Suddenly Ginny halts and calls to Susie. "Susie, stop. If Daddy catches that chain off the hook…I have a feeling it would be worse for me than that vision in the barn."

Susie stares at Ginny for a moment, then says, "I doubt that. Now you're the crazy one! God, me and my stupid ideas!"

Susie and Ginny race to the barn door and they struggle to get the chain and lock back on. As soon as the lock clicks, they run, holding hands, into an adjacent field and stop under a grove of Osage orange trees. They start catching their breaths until an Osage orange fruit falls to the ground, barely missing Susie's head.

"I get out of the barn," Susie says, "only to be killed by some ugly green fruit? Somebody up there, give me a break."

Ginny, who is still out of breath, speaks between gasps. "Better…get out…from under these trees."

They rise and find a thicket of sycamores and oaks and sit on a limestone rock in the middle of the thicket. Susie's breathing is near normal now, and Ginny is jealous of Susie having the discipline to stay in shape. She could have gotten in shape working on the farm, but Daddy said that was "man's work" and wouldn't let her join in.

"Guess we know how your grandfather died," Susie says. "Jesus Christ, that's like hell come to earth. No wonder your father's nuts."

Ginny slows her breathing, holding her hand over her heart. "You about made me have a heart attack by convincing me to get inside that barn. You were so close to being haunted for eternity by my ghost. I would come at the worst times, too, like when you're with one of your boyfriends."

"I'm sure you'd find that entertaining," Susie says. "It would definitely be..." Susie pauses, and takes a sensual breath "...exciting."

Ginny's voice turns sharp. "As for excitement, you know what happens to girls like you in horror movies. And don't insult my daddy, either."

"Well, excuse me," Susie says. "I pull you up to help you out of the barn, a stray fruit almost took off my head, and you fuss at me."

"Going inside the barn was your idea."

"Well, you went along, and you found out what happened to your grandfather, too." Susie laughs.

Ginny looks at her incredulously. "How can you laugh after...that?"

Susie keeps laughing. "Because we sound like little kids arguing. Anyway, I *need* to laugh."

Ginny smiles, hugs Susie and kisses her on the cheek. Although Ginny is smiling outwardly, inwardly her body quakes with fear. Her smile turns into a frown.

"I don't feel like laughing," Ginny says. "I don't know why we had that vision or what kept us from moving. It's like some memory of what happened that's stored in the barn. I don't want to go back there. I'm scared to live here. No wonder Daddy struggles. Please don't call him crazy. My daddy's acting strange 'cause this crazy place is confusing him."

*Confusing him is an understatement*, Ginny thinks. *Susie's right; Daddy has been acting crazy. That's a family matter, and Susie should not butt in, at least for now. But if things get worse...*

Ginny prays that Daddy won't worsen. She hears

rumors from time to time that her granddaddy and great-granddaddy were criminally insane. Sometimes elderly people down the road shut their doors when she walks by or rides by on her bike. These same neighbors are nice to Daddy and seem to respect him, but there are whispers about a family curse. Ginny shivers, wondering what would be worse; remaining in ignorance about a curse or discovering that it is true - and that its nature is pure horror.

Susie's sigh interrupts Ginny's thoughts. She tells Ginny, "I'll try to be careful, but I'm not sure you're right. Your father seems crazier than hell."

Ginny frowns. *Daddy has been more than odd lately. It's like something else is controlling him. I'd better take it easy on Susie.* "I understand," Ginny says. "But Susie..."

Susie frowns. "Okay, I see that look on your face. I get the message. I'm sorry I called your father nuts. Should I sew my mouth shut? We tight?"

They make fists and strike them against one another. Ginny smiles and says, "We tight. And don't sew your mouth shut. At least not yet."

They sit in silence, and a breeze returns to waft the leaves above them, stirring dappled shadows into shifting waves of grey and white. The moving air brushes their hair into lawless patterns, and Ginny considers today's chaos and wonders what Paul would say about it. She imagines Paul at school, playing chess with his friends, leaving his game to talk to her. Just as something interesting is about to happen in her daydream, Susie interrupts, and the pleasant image passes into the surrounding shadows.

"Did anything weird happen in the house?"

"You just interrupted a wonderful daydream," Ginny says.

"About Paul, I suppose."

Ginny ignores the reference to Paul. "The house? No, never anything weird. Maybe the barn is all we have to worry about. As long as we keep out everything should be okay."

"Sounds like good advice," Susie says. "But what if we stirred something up that escaped?"

"Please," Ginny says. "One worry at a time."

Susie bows her head, then looks at Ginny and says, "Somebody ought to build a fence around that damn barn."

Ginny shakes her head. "Daddy would be the one to do that. I won't ask him now given the way he's been acting. If I told him the reason why, he'd say I was getting visions from Satan and need to repent. So I guess that means no fence. God help anybody else who gets inside that barn."

# CHAPTER 3

Ginny tries to sleep that night, but every time she falls asleep a nightmare jolts her awake. What scares her most is that the same nightmare repeats over and over. In the dream, Ginny is inside the barn. It is dim, with a ghostly grey light illuminating the floor in front of the hole. A figure rises from the abyss, its face shrouded in shadow. It floats toward Ginny and stops in front of her until they stand face to face. She struggles to move, to turn her head, to close her eyes, but she is paralyzed.

The figure starts to peel away the shadows hiding its face as if it were pulling off sunburned skin. Slick, bright, blood-red splotches, the same color as the barn, appear in the places where the being's skin used to be. Its head is bald. Two pointed ears, twisted, deformed, protrude from the skull.

The ears are too small for the head. Two horns emerge from the top, goat-like and blood red. The flat nose appears syphilitic, eaten away, leaving two gaping wounds like a human skull after the skin has rotted off. Ginny's stomach lurches as she imagines rancid filth spewing from the beast's mouth along with the stench of sulfur and rotting flesh.

The beast peels the shadows from its mouth. Abnormally large lips appear, and they are curved upward in a permanent sarcastic smile. There are no teeth. The closest parallel Ginny can imagine is the horrid Greek comedy mask, the one with the perpetual, fixed grin. She recalls the first time she saw it, staring out at her from the pages of her sixth grade social studies book. She had slammed the book closed and shoved it off her desk. It scared her then, and it scares her now. The image still haunts her dreams, but in this lucid dream - for she realizes it is a dream — somehow she knows there is something real and rotten behind it.

The beast starts to speak, though its lips stay unmoving. The voice reminds her of someone spitting tobacco juice into a can. When she was a little girl, she saw two of her great uncles chew tobacco when they visited. She would cover her eyes or turn away to avoid puking. Now she is nauseated and hopes that nausea does not extend to her sleeping body.

The beast says, "Well, well. Here's Ginny, the goody-goody girl."

The voice changes into Sheldon's voice. "You're going to hell, rebellious daughter! Soon. Very soon."

The demon's face draws nearer and waves back and forth like the faces of people dreaming in old movies. Ginny tries to scream, but her mouth refuses to open. She wills a voice inside her head to shout, "Wake up! Wake up!"

Her eyes fly open. She is in her own bed. Her heart attempts to beat itself out of her chest. She fears it will burst from the strain. With an act of sheer will she forces her breathing to even out. She calms her thoughts. "What in the name of all that is holy was that?" she ponders. "Just a dream, or something more? A warning? Is something bad going to happen to Daddy? Is something bad going to happen to me? I should tell Daddy; but he'll only accuse me of messing with the occult."

She could hear her father's voice in her head. "Dreams can't foretell the future anymore. That only happened in Bible times. The age of miracles is over!"

She will keep a close eye on Daddy, and she will be careful. She decides that the demon in her dream is a symbol of whatever mental illness is afflicting Daddy.

Ginny is afraid that Daddy will hit her. Three months ago, after she stayed out too late at Susie's house, he balled up his fist, and Ginny cringed as she readied herself to duck. Sheldon's fingers relaxed, but he banned her from seeing Susie for two weeks. She and Susie would meet in the woods when Daddy was plowing, but Ginny was deathly afraid she would be caught and said a prayer of thanks when the ban period passed. She plans to pray a lot more in the future.

Ginny sleeps for two more hours. When her alarm goes off at six, she slams it and mutters, "Oh, no. Not morning already." Time for breakfast and another battle with Daddy. That's how it's been the last six months. She took a bath the previous night, so she dresses, dabs on only minimal makeup lest she offend Daddy, who finds makeup vain, and walks downstairs to the kitchen.

The Sprigg kitchen is cramped, with an electric stove, an older model refrigerator, and a small, plain wood table covered by a slick plastic tablecloth. Sheldon sits in a varnished wooden chair at the table. He is tall and stocky but not obese. His hair is jet-black, not auburn like Ginny's, and he's wearing overalls. Elma sits between Ginny and Sheldon. Before them is a breakfast of bacon, eggs and milk.

*Beats cereal*, Ginny thinks, thanking God for small favors.

They bow their heads as Sheldon gives the blessing. "Holy Father, we thank Thee for this food and all the blessings of this life. Help us always to obey Thy holy will and not sin against Thee. In Jesus' name, A-men."

They begin to eat. Although Ginny hates to bring up meeting Susie because of her daddy's reaction, she knows that he will ban them for life from visiting one another if she goes to Susie's and fails to tell her parents. She smiles, takes a deep breath, and speaks.

"Susie invited me to dinner tonight. We're going to study together for Mrs. Markhard's algebra test. We'll probably be the only two that pass."

Mrs. Markhard's class fits her name. That battle ax is the hardest teacher in Morhollow High. Rumor has it that she fails more than half her class. Her style is pure intimidation; students must write their homework answers on the board and wait in dread for Mrs. Markhard's latest version of sarcasm.

Old lady Markhard was the only teacher to ever drive Susie to tears. *"Miss Cottrell, your brain is a frozen turd,"* she had pronounced from on high after Susie wrote an obviously incorrect answer on the board. Susie burst into tears and fled the classroom. The class had blessed relief with a substitute until Mrs. Markhard finished her two-week suspension without pay. The school board would have fired her except for her thirty-five years of tenure. You'd figure she would learn. Although she never used coarse language in class again, she was meaner than ever and seemed to delight in clever insults. "Ms. Sprigg," she told Ginny a month after Susie's debacle, "your neurons are twigs; very *short* twigs." Ginny stifled tears. No one in the class dared to giggle. They knew eventually they would all be in the same boat.

Mrs. Markhard is the only teacher at Morhollow High who assigns homework due on the day of a test. That's because she only allows the class 25 minutes to take the test, with the last half of the class devoted to the usual homework hell. It is like having a double dose of hell the same day.

"Well, I suppose two heads are better than one when it comes to studying." Sheldon's grudging response shatters Ginny's reverie, drawing her attention back to the breakfast table. "I knew Molly Markhard in school. If the devil had a girlfriend, it would be her. I pity you for having her as your teacher." Ginny nibbles a strip of crisp bacon.

*So far, so good*, Ginny thinks. Then she stops thinking and regrets what she says as soon as it escapes her mouth. "Susie's so outgoing. I heard she has two dates for the school dance next Saturday."

On seeing the frown on Daddy's face, Ginny knows right away that she blew it. To Daddy, using the word *dance* is like dropping an f-bomb. Ginny cringes, waiting for the inevitable storm.

Sheldon raises his voice, as Ginny expected. "Be sure you stay away from dances. Church wouldn't appreciate the preacher's daughter behaving like no harlot."

*Whew,* Ginny thinks. *That was close.* She passes a plate of bacon to Sheldon. "Don't worry so much, Daddy. I don't have time to go to dances."

Ginny believes this is an innocent comment, until Sheldon reaches across the table, grabs Ginny's shoulders and glares at her. His face is bright red, blood-red - like the barn. *What in the world did I say now?* Ginny asks herself.

"Not having time is not a good enough reason," Sheldon intones in the sacrosanct voice that drives Ginny nuts. "You don't go to dances because you want to obey God, not because you *don't have time.* God demands absolute obedience. Anything less, and He'll send you straight to hell. I love you too much, my child, to let you suffer."

*'My child,' my ass,* Ginny thinks, and hopes her thoughts don't escape her mind and leave her mouth. Ginny feels a surge of anger rising and bites her lip before she says something she knows she would regret.

Thankfully, Elma stands up and defends Ginny for a change. "Don't be so hard on Ginny. She said she's not goin'."

*Good for you, Mama,* Ginny thinks, praying that Daddy will calm down rather than pick a fight. That would turn a Mrs. Markhard-double-dose-of-hell day into a triple-dose day.

Sheldon extends his arms, hands down, and lowers them slowly as if quietening a crowd. He sighs and shrugs his shoulders. "I'm sorry, Ginny. I'm worried about you. Old devil's after you. After us all."

Elma starts putting dishes into the dishpan. Ginny gets up to help. She then says something that reveals that she is just as stupidly bold as Susie. She turns her head toward Sheldon, laughs, and says, "You worry too much about the devil. Like you're obsessed."

*Stupid, stupid, stupid!* Ginny knows as soon as she closes her mouth. *Too late - this will be bad.* She imagines her head changing into the head of a braying jackass. Elma stops doing the dishes and looks sharply at Ginny.

"Ginny, watch it!" she says, but the damage is done. Sheldon stands up, towering over Ginny, and points at her. He shouts and gesticulates in a way that reminds Ginny of old newsreel footages of Hitler she saw in history class.

"Don't call me obsessed, demon-child," Sheldon says. "You're gettin' an attitude, and I don't like it. It's my job to raise you to obey God's commandments."

That does it for Ginny. Her stomach sinks as all emotional control flows out of her body, and a surge of adrenalin flows in. She shrieks out her words. "Obey! Obey! That's all you talk about. God wants us to *obey*! If God's so good, why'd he let Granddaddy kill himself?"

Elma's face pales, and her voice changes to a harsh whisper. "How did you... Ginny, stop that now!"

Sheldon walks rapidly toward Ginny, his red, arterial blood turning his face purple like venous blood. Fury twists his features into a frowning demon. Elma whispers, "Oh no, here we go..."

Sheldon yells at the top of his voice. "How do you know how my daddy really died? The devil tell you? Stop blaspheming! Go to your room! Now! When you're ready to apologize for what you said about your Maker, I *may* let you visit your friend Susie tonight."

Ginny no longer cares what she says. "You promised, you bastard. Don't you think promise-breaking is wrong, hypocrite? Go to hell!"

Sheldon pauses, his face twisting into a furrowed red thing. Elma steps toward Sheldon and Ginny and yells, "Ginny! Stop that talk right now. You ain't making it any easier on yourself."

Sheldon towers over Ginny and raises his hand to slap her, but she ducks under his arm and runs toward the kitchen door. Sheldon starts to follow her, but Elma blocks him. Sheldon pushes her out of the way and swings at Ginny with his outstretched palm, striking her on the right side of her face. She screams and runs away. Elma grabs Sheldon by the arm. He turns around and raises his fist.

Elma involuntarily holds her hands in front of her face and shrieks, "Sheldon, Stop!"

He stops, his fist still raised, his face flushed, his eyes looking like they will pop out any moment. "Ginny was wrong," Elma calms her voice and says, "I'll talk to her. But you had no call to raise your hand like that. Ginny's too old for a whippin,' and you had no business slapping her face."

Sheldon's face furrows further as if someone tilled his face with a deformed blade. "Get out of my way, shrew. If I don't punish her severely she'll burn in hell like my father is burning for killing himself." Sheldon's fist remains suspended in midair as if between two worlds.

Elma looks at Sheldon eye to eye and says, "You

ain't the judge. You don't know what went through your daddy's mind. He might have been crazier than a chicken drunk on moonshine and didn't have any idea of what he was doing. If God can't forgive a man for what he can't help, we're all doomed to hell. You, too, despite your high-falutin' thinking that you're better than anybody else. Now you ain't been acting right, and you'd better tell me the reason. Beatenist thing I've ever seen."

Sheldon lowers his fists, shakes his head vigorously, and says, "I have not been acting strange. I have obeyed God more fully than at any other time in my life. You'd better take care to do the same."

"You are going crazy," Elma says. "You ain't showing no mercy. Lordy, I sure would hate for you to be Jesus. We'd all be going to hell but you. Wouldn't it get lonely up there, living all by yourself?"

Sheldon raises his hand, then lowers it, shrugs his shoulders and huffs a breathy "uhhh" sound. He storms out the kitchen door. A moment later, the front door to the house slams.

# CHAPTER 4

Ginny lies down in her bed, her head a pressure cooker of steam. *Daddy has gone way to far,* she fumes. *Obedience is all well and good, but without love and kindness, obedience is just a sandwich without the bread.*

Ginny laughs at the image, remembering the carb-free hamburger she tried at Hardees without reading the description on the menu board. "Where's the bread?" she said, when the burger arrived wrapped in lettuce. Susie fell out of her chair laughing, and the customers at a nearby table complained to the management about "chattering teenagers."

The memory helps to calm her ire. She focuses on getting ready to catch the school bus. Her mind wanders. *Daddy didn't object to me seeing Susie except when he threw that tantrum. That means he won't change his mind at suppertime tonight. He's so strict with himself that he'd say since he didn't try to stop this visit, he'd be going back on his word if he said otherwise. As if going back on his word,* Ginny thinks sarcastically, *is a sin that would send him to hell.*

*Poor Daddy.* Ginny worries about him when she's not furious with him She remembers the barn and

35

fears there is something behind her vision. Perhaps the barn is more than just a repository for evil memories. Maybe something malevolent lives there, something tormenting Daddy's mind.

After gathering her book bags, Ginny walks downstairs and out the front door toward Allenville Road, her feet crunching gravel on the drive. She turns around and stares at the barn. The barn starts to melt like the demon-face in her dream, and she stifles a scream before the sound of the school bus stopping pulls her out of the daymare. At school, she moves as if in a daze as she struggles to strike that demonic image from her mind. The monotonous drone of her teachers' voices in successive class calms her nerves. By the time she gets home she feels nearly back to normal.

Daddy says nothing at supper that evening. He stares blankly ahead as if in a trance. Ginny reasons that the best thing to do is behave as normally as possible, and immediately after helping Mama with the dishes she tells her she is leaving for Susie's. If Sheldon objects, he does not show it, his eyes staring blankly into something; Ginny knows not what.

The stifling humidity worsens in the early evening, and Ginny wipes the beads of sweat off her brow, a flash of anger striking at Daddy's refusal to let her wear shorts, though it's not like they'd help much with this stickiness. Her shirt cleaves to her skin, and she imagines Paul appreciating the view. Then she feels the flush of heat flow across her face. The mixture of thrill and shame from having such a thought entices.

She passes blooming orange day lilies dotting the ditch by the road. As much as possible she stays in the shade made by oaks and a few hickory trees. Their branches overhang the road and help block a sun that stays late in the sky during daylight savings time. Ginny starts as a black cat leaps out into the road, halts in front of her, and screams like a banshee before it flies into the brush. Ginny nearly screams herself, but the familiar site of the Harris Farms Subdivision where Susie Cottrell lives calms her.

The houses in Harris Farms are small by McMansion standards but are still roomy enough for most families. Monica Cottrell and Susie live in a red-brick, ranch-style house with a small concrete porch, typical of older subdivisions. Ginny steps up to the front door and knocks. The door opens, and Susie's mother, Monica, appears. She has passed the big 4-0, but could still pass for 35, blond like Susie, slender, and neatly dressed. *Why would Monica's husband Jack run off on her with a young floosy?* Ginny thinks. *Maybe he thought she would make him young again. Men are so stupid sometimes. At least Paul is not that way.*

Monica smiles and extends her arms to hug Ginny. "Ginny!" she says. "Come in. Susie's in her room but I'm sure you can coax her into the den."

Ginny walks past the kitchen; a crucifix hangs on the wall, an odd site to Ginny. Her mind wanders back to a conversation with Sheldon. *Daddy said Jesus shouldn't be hanging on a crucifix since God raised him from the dead. But isn't it more appropriate to have an image of Christ in one's home rather than a Bible enshrined prominently on a table? Aren't Christians supposed to worship Jesus instead of a book, however holy that book might be?*

Ginny moves down a hallway into Susie's room,

where Susie is sitting on her bed. She stands up, hugs Ginny and says, "Mother, we need to have some girl talk."

Monica smiles and says, "All right, girls. Join me in the den later, 'kay?"

Monica shuts the door behind her as she leaves. Susie motions Ginny to the bed to sit. She turns her head toward Ginny, about to talk, but stops as she stares at her face.

"What? Did I grow warts?" Ginny asks.

Susie shakes her head. "No. Sorry. You just look really worn out. Is anything wrong? Another fight with your Dad?"

Ginny tears up. "It was awful. I was stupid. I said things I should have known would set him off, then I got so mad I didn't care what I said. Daddy tried to slap me, but I ducked. Then he swung his arm again— and this time he connected. I'm proud of Mama, though. She stood up to him for a change, though she's mad at me for calling him a bastard and telling him to go to hell."

Susie frowns. "Slapping you at your age is attempted child abuse. You have every right to phone the police."

"That's just severe discipline, though, and even if it were abuse I wouldn't have called the sheriff's office."

Susie huffs and says, "I don't know what you people down here call discipline, but where I live your father's behavior would land him in jail. If he slaps you again, hits you with his fists, or strikes your mother, you need to call the cops, period."

"Let's hope that doesn't happen."

"I 'spose one can hope," Susie says, sounding

skeptical. There is a moment of silence. Susie's face transforms, taking on the features of a cat that is about to torment a cornered mouse. Her voice takes a more cheerful tone. "Hey, you need a break. Let's go somewhere tonight - and I don't mean the library."

"I don't like the look on your face," Ginny says. "What is it you want us to do? We'll go to the library later, right? I have to study for this test and finish my homework – and so do you."

"Of course we'll go to the library—or we can come back here and study. We can sit on the porch. I have bug repellent in the car to keep the mosquitoes away."

"Where do you want to go first?" Ginny asks.

"Wait and see."

Ginny rolls her eyes. "Yeah, right."

Ginny and Susie walk down the hall into the living room, open a door, and descend downstairs to an attractive basement den. Two bookcases line the wall to their left. An electric fireplace is at the back. On a round wooden table on the right side Jack Daniels appears to be having a pleasant conversation with Jim Beam, while Jose Cuervo and Captain Morgan look on. By the table is a small refrigerator. Monica walks in with glasses filled with ice and says, "Cola and Diet Cola are in the fridge. Don't you girls even think about the other drinks."

Susie rolls her eyes. "You just made us think about them by saying that. Come on, Mom. We could at least have a glass of wine."

Ginny sputters as she speaks. "But Daddy and Mama wouldn't..."

"That makes it even more out of the question," Monica says. "I'm not going to offend Mr. and Mrs.

Sprigg. And Susie, don't roll your eyes at me if you know what's good for your date nights."

Susie puts her hands on her hips and takes an exasperated breath. "Mother. Don't mess with my se,.. I mean, my dates. As for Ginny's father, he offends..."

Monica moves directly in front of Susie and interrupts. "That's enough, Susie," she says. "I don't think Ginny appreciates your talking about her parents that way."

Ginny blushes but stays silent.

Monica stands back and says, "You two can chat here before you go to the library. Remember, Susie, the *library*. That's what you promised me. You'll both want to do well on that big algebra test. Especially you, Susie."

Susie exhales hard, her lips forming a pout. Then her shoulders slump and she says, "Okay, okay."

Monica leaves. As soon as her footsteps are no longer heard, Susie laughs. Ginny half-smiles, but feels wary. *Susie is good overall, but she has that cat-like mischievous streak that drives me crazy. Whenever I go along with that streak, I get in trouble. But Susie can be so darned persistent.*

Susie returns to her conspiratorial tone of voice. "Now Ginny, I'll tell you what I really have in mind. Since we can still study later, you wouldn't be exactly lying to your parents. All you have to say is that we met to study and not give them other information."

Ginny raises her eyebrows. "What kind of *other information?*"

"Well," Susie says, "those library study rooms are sooooo boring; and we would be cramped there. A room probably won't be open on the eve of Mrs. Markhard's test."

"I guess we'll have to study here," Ginny says.

Susie says, "Like I said. We will. Soon enough. Now we need to loosen up before we study. Have some fun."

Ginny folds her arms and asks, "What kind of fun?"

Susie answers. "I know a bar outside of town. The owner doesn't care about how old you are if you want to drink. Hell, he'd serve a whiskey to a two-year-old."

Ginny's voice turns cold. "You know that's wrong. Daddy says alcohol kills brain cells. He says even one drink is the first drink on the road to hell."

Susie wrings her hands. "Hell, hell, hell - that's all your father can talk about. Plus, that's bullshit about the brain cells. That's a lie Fundamentalist churches tell to keep people from drinking. Maybe, like, if you get drunk all the time it will fry your brain, but not for most people who drink. Jesus drank wine, so drinking's cool, right, since Jesus is cool?"

"But that was really grape juice," Ginny says.

Susie bursts out laughing. "Are you kidding? In those days grape juice would have turned to wine overnight. I bet your stupid father told you that grape juice bull."

Ginny raises her voice. Daddy is a jerk lately, but her best friend's so obviously despising him is beyond the pale. "You know I've never liked you talking about Daddy that way," she says. "Just because your d..."

Susie turns away. Her body shakes with sobs. Ginny feels sick. If her foot could reach far enough she'd give herself a good kick in the mouth to stop it from running away. Her face turns deeply red and she lowers her head. "I'm sorry Susie. It was terrible of me to bring that up. Can you forgive me?"

Susie pulls out a Kleenex from her purse and wipes her eyes and speaks through sobs. "The bitch he ran off with is ugly as sin. Why would Dad leave Mom for that?"

Ginny keeps her head down and speaks in a low voice. "I guess looks don't always matter to some men. I won't say anything about it again. I swear."

"Well," Susie says, recovering her usual cheerful voice, "I'm sorry for insulting your father again. It's just that some of what he believes is du..., I mean, it is strange to me. I guess we're even on saying stupid stuff. We'll pretend none of this happened. Now raise your head or I'll force it up with a car jack."

Ginny brushes away her remaining tears with her hand and hugs Susie. Then she asks, "What's so fun about a bar?"

Susie breaks the hug and stands back, her smile returning. "How to have fun at a bar?" she says. "Are you kidding? There's great loud music, good looking guys, and that wonderful warm feeling from the drinks. Try one drink. Just one. You'll see. One drink doesn't mean you're an alcoholic."

"I don't know," Ginny says. "If my folks ever found out. Especially Daddy."

Susie has that look on her face that Ginny knows is a sign of cocksureness. Warning bells ring in her head, and for a moment she remembers Edgar Allen Poe's poem, "The Bells." The thought tickles her, and she stifles a giggle. She looks again at Susie's face and starts to titter, but she turns her head away and clears her throat.

Susie smiles broadly, her perfect teeth showing.

"Your folks will never know. You'll come home in time for his silly curfew - 10:30! By then he won't even smell any liquor on your breath. I have some breath mints that would hide a half-day's worth of drinking. They always work for me. As far as your father knows, you were his little sweet studious angel."

A surge of frustration rises inside Ginny. *I'm going to regret this. Daddy will find out. He always does. When this "this will happen for sure" message comes into my mind, I'm usually right. Daddy might find out what I did by hearing gossip around town. People will see Susie at the bar, and someone may recognize her. Lately, the way words slip off her over-slick tongue, she might give away the secret herself. But I don't want to disappoint her. I suppose I'll humor her one more time.* Ginny sighs and speaks halfheartedly. "Okay, but only once. Because you're my friend."

Susie jumps up like an over-enthused sports fan and raises her arms into the air, looking like she's signaling a touchdown. "Shoot, yeah, girl! We'll have a great time, I promise."

Ginny nods, smiles, and stands up. *I'll try to have fun,* she thinks. *If I'm going to get in trouble anyway, I might as well enjoy it.*

They step outside into Monica's car, a sporty model she bought for Susie, but had to use as her own when her husband left with their new minivan. Ginny's stomach turns with revulsion. *I know what happens in the back of the minivan, at least until those two adulterers get tired of one other. I know Susie thinks this car is hers, but Monica is overly permissive in lending it to Susie as often as she does. Between Susie's dates and our visits, I don't know how Monica has the car long enough to make a trip to the grocery store? Life has its mysteries.*

They get inside the car, and Susie plays a CD of AC-DC. Oldies but goodies, although Daddy would slap Ginny down to China if he knew one of the songs on the CD is "Highway to Hell."

They ride past the old downtown part of Morhollow to the gravel parking lot of a decrepit bar. The building is run down, with slats of siding hanging off the bottom, and the building hasn't been painted in a long time. There are, though, some bright, colorful lights the owner strung up by the door along with illuminated signs with the brand names of various beers stamped on them. Ginny and Susie walk around the building to the door as Ginny looks over the group of Harleys parked side by side in the lot.

Ginny moves closer to Susie and asks, "Are there rough people inside?"

"What? Just because of the motorcycles outside? These guys are like big teddy bears. One time they rescued a dog that had been hit by a car and took him to the vet. They saved his life. Anyway, there are more than motorcycle club people in here. Relax. You'll love it."

Above the door is a sign: BUD'S PLACE. Susie opens the door, and a swaying man keeps it open for them, smiles leeringly, and Susie and Ginny walk in. Loud honky tonk music plays - Hank Williams, Jr. Susie takes Ginny's hand and walks her to the counter. The bartender, Jack, is in his fifties and wearing overalls. His beard consists of rough stubble, and he reminds Susie of the bartender on Tatooine in the first (or was it the fourth?) *Star Wars* movie. Susie leans over the counter and kisses Jack on the cheek. Ginny's stomach turns and she looks away, studying the Christmas-like lights above her head and trying not to choke on the cigarette smoke.

Susie speaks above the crowd noise. "Hi, Jack. How's my favorite bartender?"

"Pretty damn good after that kiss," Jack says. "Who's that nice young thang you came with tonight?" Ginny blushes and lowers her head, as much from disgust as embarrassment. She says, "I'm Ginny."

Jack looks her over a bit too much for comfort, and for once Ginny is grateful for Daddy's dress code. "You sure are perty," says Jack, and Ginny stifles a wave of nausea. Jack continues. "What you havin' tonight?"

*Having? What am I supposed to have? Do they serve Coke at bars? They must. What about other non-sinful drinks - water, iced tea, fruit juices, or non-alcoholic grape juice like the church uses at the Lord's Supper? The only beers I've seen are on a TV screen or on the front of Alfred Culbertson's porch, where he stacks his mini-cities of used cans.*

A part of her understands Daddy's concern. Mr. Culbertson was once a respected business owner who ran a local clothing store, but when hard times forced him to close the store, he started to drink. He only exists as an alcoholic shell now.

Ginny considered asking for a Diet Coke or a glass of water, but the look on Susie's face said that wasn't an option. Against her better judgment, she lets Susie decide.

Susie points her thumb at Ginny. "She'll have a

Michelob Lite. I'll have the usual."

"Comin' right up," Jack says, the slur in his voice worsening. *I reckon he enjoys a few drinks while on duty and is in the process of enjoying more,* Ginny thinks. *Wonder if Bud, the owner, knows—unless Jack is Bud or "Bud" refers to Budweiser.*

Ginny pulls some money out of her purse to pay her bill, but Susie laughs and says, "Be shy, I buy, girl. I asked Jack to put us on the same tab." Ginny is so nervous she forgets to thank Susie.

Jack brings Ginny her beer. "Thanks," Ginny says to Jack, holding the glass gingerly as if it were a vial of poison. "You're welcome, little girl," Jack says, and Ginny wonders if she can drink anything after he said that. Susie stares at her a moment, smiling. "Come on, take a sip," she says. "Try it!"

Ginny takes a big gulp instead of a sip. She gags and coughs, but manages to keep the beer down. Susie laughs loudly, and Jack smiles as he brings Susie her drink. Susie raises her glass and says "Cheers." Ginny knows enough from TV to click glasses and return the proper reply. "Cheers."

"Com'on. Drink up!" Susie says, a bit too loudly for Ginny's liking. Ginny shakes her head vigorously. No way would she drink more of that sh..., that crap. She figures if poop tastes like anything, she's probably just tasted it. Susie pats Ginny on the shoulder.

"It's okay. You have to get used to the taste. No one likes beer the first time they try it. I'm going to enjoy my screwdriver."

"Screwdriver?" Ginny asks.

Susie laughs again. "I'll explain it later."

# CHAPTER 5

Sheldon Sprigg sleeps fitfully, his body twisting and turning. Elma is on her side, sleeping soundly beside him. Sheldon gets up and saunters to a small desk, flips a switch to a desk lamp, the light of which he blocks on one side with a piece from a cardboard box so as not to disturb Elma. On the desk lies an open Bible.

Six months ago, Sheldon visited his daddy's grave for the first time in the many years since he hanged himself. There Sheldon prayed that he would be a better daddy than his, and that he would do his best to keep Ginny out of hell. As soon as he finished praying, a rushing mighty wind struck him like a force field, and he fell flat on the ground. He heard a still, small voice whisper in his ear. He was convinced — and remains convinced — that this was the voice of God, speaking to him as he spoke to Elijah in the wilderness in the shadowy past.

Tonight, the feeling he had by his daddy's grave is especially strong, raising the hairs on his head. There is a breath of whisper in the air, then words. "Sheldon," the singsong voice says, putting more emphasis on the first syllable. Dis-i-pline." The whisper lingers for a moment, then wafts away, as if caught on the wind.

*That's it!* he thinks, and a sliver of hope rises that he might save Ginny from her rebellious state of the past three years. *She's talked back to me and Elma and gone out with that Papist, that slutty blond Susie. Every time Ginny goes out with the Mary worshipping whore her rebellion worsens. The slut got smart with me one day, said I have "too tight of an asshole." I should slit her with a carving knife from neck to waist. That would end her nefarious influence on Ginny. That option, unfortunately, is not open; yet. So far, Jesus hasn't told me to make Ginny pay the ultimate penalty for her sins. If only God's law against killing didn't apply to Susie.*

*Lord Jesus, please let me hear your blessed voice tell me how to hold Ginny in line. She hates every moment of my discipline, but it's only for the best reason of all; to keep her soul out of hell and allow her to enter into the joy of her Lord.*

*Lord, can't you be specific? How should I discipline Ginny? Is there any hope for her soul, some balm in Gilead? Reassure me, Lord Jesus. Don't let her be like Daddy, who now burns in everlasting fire for choosing death over the life you graciously gave him. I can't bear for Ginny to join Daddy, suffering forever, skin burning, blisters and boils forming, and my beloved daughter screaming and crying. in eternal fire. Give me a sign, O Lord!*

Sheldon stands beside the open window, waiting for God to speak again. A breeze tousles his hair. He folds his arms tightly and shivers. The breeze continues to blow, riffling through the pages of his open Bible. Sheldon gasps as the breeze dies down, and the pages stop turning.

*Lord, is this Your sign? This must be a sign!*

The Bible is opened to the first chapter of II Thessalonians in the New Testament. A sharp red glow highlights part of the page, and Sheldon reads out loud.

"And to you who are troubled rest with us, when the Lord Jesus shall be revealed from heaven with his mighty angels, in flaming fire taking vengeance on them that know not God, and that obey not the gospel of our Lord Jesus Christ: who shall be punished with everlasting destruction from the presence of the Lord, and from the glory of his power."

Sheldon stumbles to a chair, hyperventilating. He whispers to himself, "This has to be about Ginny. She won't listen to me. She is running further from God every day. She constantly disobeys God and is disrespectful to me. I have to do something to save her soul from everlasting torment in hell. Lord, I beg you, show me how to save her."

A bright, white light from outside streams through the window, illuminating the room. Sheldon peeks out the window. The light seems to have its source in the barn. Sheldon laughs out loud, then stifles the laugh and whispers. "Yes! A sign! Lord! Oh Lord! Tell me how to save my Ginny!"

Sheldon runs downstairs, out the back door and into the yard. He walks toward the barn but covers his eyes as the light grows brighter. He falls to the ground and speaks into the red clay earth that smells like a freshly plowed garden in the cool of the night. He begins to pray.

"Lord, I am dust compared to thee. Forgive me.

Help me, Thy unworthy servant, to save Ginny, my only child. Thou knowest I have lost Daddy to eternal torment. Don't let me lose Ginny."

Sheldon's eyes remain closed, and he does not see the being coalesce in the light. It is humanoid in shape and blood-red in color like the barn. Its thick arms have wrinkled hands that end in sharp claws. The body is covered with scales that steam with smoke. If the beast were not humanoid someone might label it as a dragon. Curved, goat-like horns and small ears appear on each side of its hairless head. It has no teeth, but its lips are abnormally wide, the mouth perpetually open in a mocking smile.

Smoke hides the being for a few seconds, and when the smoke clears a figure appears who looks like a stereotypical painting of Jesus Christ: long, dark hair, white, seamless robe, and sandals. A bright glow surrounds the body and a halo appears over its head. The light fades, and Sheldon raises his head. He immediately swoons, and the figure lifts him to his feet and smiles.

"Sheldon Sprigg," the creature says, using exactly the same still, small voice Sheldon heard by his daddy's grave.

Sheldon's head is slightly bowed, his eyes closed. He feels as nothing before Christ his God. He speaks in a voice that approaches a groan. "Oh Lord, I can't gaze upon at your face. It's too bright."

The being that looks like Jesus says, "I must adjust my appearance so that you are able to look at me without dying. I have seen your home and have compassion for you in your struggles. How I can help you with...Ginny?"

Sheldon opens his eyes and extends his arms, as if

pleading. "Thank you, Jesus. Ginny doesn't want to obey you. My wife takes up for the girl. I know Thou hast seen all of this."

The false Jesus says, "You can call me 'You'. No need to talk to me like Mary Tudor. As for Ginny, things are far worse with her than you realize." He places his hands on Sheldon's head.

Sheldon's eyes fill with tears, and he snuffles out the words, "What has she done now?"

The creature's voice grows deeper and louder, a trumpet sounding out the wrath of God. "Tonight," he says, "when Ginny was supposed to be studying, she went to a bar with her evil friend, Susie."

Sheldon looks up at "Jesus" and holds his hands to his head, shaking his head as in denial. "Ginny? Drinking?"

The phony Jesus' voice remains deep, and more than a tinge of anger is present. "Do you doubt my word?" he asks.

Sheldon pales, bows to the creature, and says, "No, Lord! I never doubt you. Forgive me if it seemed that way. What can I do to save Ginny's soul?"

The Creature replies, "You must punish her so severely she will remember never to disobey me - or you - again. If Elma gets in the way, you must be a man and stand up to her. As to how severely you punish Ginny, you can use your best judgment — unless things get worse. You have been far too lenient."

*I have been too lenient, even these past six months,* Sheldon thinks. *Elma interferes due to her mushy heart. Her meddling will cause Ginny to lose her soul, and Elma will damn herself for failing to train Ginny in the nurture and admonition of the Lord. I'll end up losing both Ginny and Elma to Satan's fold if I fail the task my Lord gave me.*

"Forgive me for my past leniency, Lord," Sheldon says. "I have failed thus far as a father. I won't fail Ginny, nor will I fail You again. She will never forget what I have in store for her. Never. I promise, Lord."

"Good," the creature says. "You will see me again. Go inside, and don't look back. Remember Lot's wife."

Sheldon turns and walks toward his back door. He takes care not to look behind him. Lot's wife looked back toward Sodom and Gomorrah and changed into a pillar of salt. Sheldon is so focused on not looking back that he fails to see the stumbling block right in front of him. He sprawls to the ground, rolling to his side with his face directly toward *Jesus*. He clamps his eyes shut, wildly praying for mercy that he might not be consumed in fire and brimstone. He gets up, lowers his head, turns around, and starts toward the house again. He leaps and yelps like a toy poodle when the reflection of his face in a puddle startles him.

"Jesus Christ!" Sheldon curses. He immediately bows his head and prays, "Forgive me, Lord. I did not mean to use Thy name — *Your* name — in vain."

Sheldon brushes straw and dirt off his back, shakes his head, opens the back door of the house, and steps inside.

# CHAPTER 6

As soon as the door closes, the imposter assumes his true demonic form. He shambles toward the barn. The lock unlocks on its own, the chains pull away, the doors swing open, and the Beast, the Prince of the Powers of the Air, Satan, steps inside. He takes one look outside and sighs. Then he says, in a rumbling, Darth Vader voice, "Sheldon, *I* am your father." He cackles and shrieks, "I am the father..." He pauses for a few seconds. "...of lies!

The doors close, the chains return to their proper place, and the lock clicks closed.

✦✦✦

Susie pulls her car into the Sprigg driveway and stops near the house. "You know you had fun," she smirks.

Ginny smiles. "I did."

Susie says, "Mom's going to birth a T-Rex if I don't get home. Later!" She starts down the driveway, but before she makes it to the road a bright light appears in the barn area. Susie stomps on the brakes, slams it into reverse and squeals the tires back to where Ginny stands, spellbound by the sight. She rolls down her window.

"What the fuck?" she says. "That light's, like, creepy. Get in the car. Now!"

Ginny turns toward the car, but stops.

"What's wrong? Get in here!"

Ginny says. "I'm worried something bad is wrong. Maybe there's a fire at the back of the house."

Susie grips the steering wheel until her knuckles turn white. She takes a deep breath, shakes her head, then gets out of the car, slamming the door behind her.

She says, "That doesn't look like a light from any fire I've seen. It feels...obscene. Like something so horrible that if you saw what was behind it you'd freeze into a block of ice."

Ginny laughs. "Now who's getting carried away?"

"I'm not going behind that house. I'm outta here."

Before Susie has a chance to turn around, Ginny grabs her arm and pulls her back. Ginny's face flushes, and her voice turns low and ominous. "Now look," she says. "I went to the bar with you. The least you can do for me as my friend is help me here."

Susie stands dumbstruck for a moment. Then she shrugs and says, "Okay, whatever. I think I'd rather you yell at me than use that low voice. Now don't get mad, but you go first."

"That's new," Ginny says. "That's the first time you've let me lead."

"I really am scared this time. You're my friend, but I wish I were anywhere but here."

Ginny raises a finger to signal, *quiet,* and leads the way as they move to the corner of the house and gaze toward the barn. Sheldon is on his knees, talking to a figure that appears to be...Jesus.

Susie's mouth drops like a drawbridge. She leans against Ginny, and Ginny feels Susie's heart race. Ginny's sure her friend won't put on a show of being brave this time. Susie says, "What the fu...?"

"Shh," Ginny whispers. "Listen."

She cups her ears with her hands. The false Jesus and Sheldon converse while Ginny's eyes widen more than ever. The false Jesus turns away from Sheldon and toward the girls. Ginny staggers back, runs into Susie, and they tumble to the ground. Susie sits up slowly and pulls Ginny into a seated position. "Gin, you okay?" she asks. "We have to split. Let's go!"

Ginny's breaths come deep and fast. She doesn't move for a moment, and Susie taps her on the shoulder and whispers in a gravely tone, "Come onnn. Let's get the hell out of here. I don't think that dude is really Jesus."

"I *know* it's not Jesus," Ginny says. "I don't know what it is. It saw me, I think. It felt dirty. Like all the evil and filth and puke in the universe combined. Like it has come to feed on us."

Susie stutters as she speaks. "Then let's go. I don't want to meet that thing face to face."

They begin to crawl around the house to the front where the porch light is on. They sit on the edge of the porch, Susie's arms around Ginny. They catch their breaths and speak in low voices.

"At least there's some real light on this porch," Susie says. That light before..."

Ginny finishes Susie's sentence. "...wasn't light at all. Anti-light. It made me feel dark, cold and alone.

That thing...that monster. I heard it speak. It told Daddy I drank at the bar with you. It watched us then. I bet it's watching us all the time, wherever we go. I bet it's watching us now."

Susie starts flapping her arms and says, "Oh crap, damn, God, what can we do?"

*There goes the last pretense of her bravery*, Ginny thinks.

Now Ginny will have to be the one pretending to be brave.

"First," Ginny says, "keep your voice down and stay calm. If Mama, or worse, Daddy, notices us, we'll have more than that Jesus-thing to worry about. I'll need to convince my parents to leave this place. Mama might listen. She's always been more open-minded than Daddy. I don't think I can convince Daddy, not now, especially since he knows I drank alcohol. If we can get him out of this place long enough, if distance helps at all, maybe Mama and I working together can convince him this beast is not Jesus. O God. I'm sure this thing is what made Daddy turn so mean."

"What are you going to tell your father, I mean, about the bar?" Susie asks.

Ginny sighs. "I don't know. Daddy's going to be after me. If I'm lucky, he'll think this night has been a dream and I didn't drink at all."

Susie looks around. "I don't see any sign of that light that weirded us out. But I'm sure your father will remember his conversation with that thing and that he's going to be super pissed. No way you'll be safe in that house. Why don't you stay with us tonight? That way you won't have to deal with your father until tomorrow morning."

Ginny shakes her head. "No, he'd be madder than

ever. The way he's been lately, he'd probably accuse your mom of kidnapping me. With those deputies he knows — and he knows quite a few of them - we both could be in deep doo doo."

Susie giggles and says, "Before long I'll have you saying "deep shit."

"Don't think so," Ginny says, and she pauses to rest her head in her hand.

"Are you sure you won't change your mind?" Susie asks.

After a few seconds Ginny replies, "No, I can't let you get into trouble for me. I'll take the risk and stay here."

"I dunno about this," says Susie. "You're stubborn, girl. Do what you have to do, but please be careful. If your father goes ape-shit, you need to run, hide, and call the cops. Whether or not you call the cops, stop by my place. Mother and I will make sure you're safe."

Ginny smiles and hugs Susie. "Don't worry. I will be careful. I'll get away if Daddy turns violent."

Ginny walks Susie to her car and hugs her goodbye. As the car's tires crunch gravel, Ginny returns to the front door, pulls out her key from her purse, and turns it as quietly as possible, opening the door. It squeaks and the floor makes too much noise as she steps into the hall. Her heart is thundering so loudly she fears her father will hear it. She makes it to the living room and the edge of the stairs. She sees her daddy around every chair, imagines his large hands sneaking around a corner to clutch her tender throat and squeeze. She imagines gagging, choking, blacking out, fading away into 'that good night.'

Ginny takes the first step on the stairs, then the

second. She's halfway up when the sound of a toilet flushing startles her. *If it's Mama,* she thinks, *she will go back to bed right away. But if it's Daddy.... he sometimes goes downstairs to the fridge to get a midnight snack.*

She freezes and squeezes her arms against her chest to quieten her quaking heart. There are footsteps. They seem to be coming toward the top of the stairs. Ginny feels faint, and her legs give way. She catches herself on the rail and lowers herself onto a step. There is a pause in the footsteps. Is that a shadow she sees at the top of the stairs? A giant, hulking shadow of a black-haired man?

She knows she's not being rational, but she moves her hands toward her eyes, wondering when Daddy's oversized hand, its muscles hewn from years of hard farm work, will seize her by the neck and squeeze, the vise grip snapping tender bones, cutting off blood and air to her brain.

The sound of the footsteps starts again, but they are moving away from the stairs. A door closes. *Good. Mama and Daddy's bedroom door,* Ginny hopes. She opens her eyes and looks upstairs. Nothing is there. *Just your silly imagination,* she thinks. She waits a few minutes for whoever went back to bed to go to sleep, and quietly scoots up the stairs. She looks to her right, then to her left when she reaches the upstairs hall. *Empty.* She crawls to her door, slips it open, and peers into darkness.

She wonders whether to take the risk of turning on the light. *What choice do I have? I knew the risks when I made the decision not to go home with Susie. Anyway, a sudden bright light will blind anyone hiding in the room.*

Ginny cracks the door the rest of the way, reaches

her bed, and pulls back the covers. She crawls under the covers and reaches for the light by the bed. She flicks the switch.

Someone is lying next to her. The body turns around slowly. Ginny can't move. Daddy must have closed her bedroom door and lay down in her bed. She imagines him springing up, hands extended, his head full of homicidal thoughts.

The head turns around so she can see it. The face is that of Jesus. Its mouth – only its mouth – starts to change shape, lips thickening, forming into an oval that twists upward into a toothless, sarcastic smile. The beast screeches with a voice like a thousand buzzards screaming at once as they land on their rotting prey. Ginny stifles a scream and shuts her eyes, immediately opening them again.

The bed is empty except for her. She gets up, looks around the room, in the closets, and under the bed. The room is, or seems, clear. Ginny does not think she'll be able to sleep in that room, but figures climbing downstairs to the couch is too risky to try. She gets dressed into her pajamas and climbs back into bed. She lies for an indeterminate time. Hours? Minutes? She has no idea. She drifts off, leaving on her lamp, the room fading into a light grey field that turns into blessed oblivion.

# CHAPTER 7

The alarm wakes Ginny up at 5:30. *Another blessed morning to shower, have a huge fight with Daddy, and get to school.* She lies on the floor and rests an ear there. She overhears her parents' voices. *All they talk about is paying bills and other boring stuff. No sign that Daddy knows about her trip to the bar. Good. He must have thought he was dreaming or forgot what happened last night.*

She can take her shower in peace. She walks into the upstairs bathroom Daddy installed six years ago since he didn't like to go downstairs to pee in the middle of the night. She undresses and turns on the cold water that serves to shock her body out of the remains of sleep. She looks down at her body. *Not bad. A flat stomach. At least my Southern country diet has not given me a beer belly without the benefit of beer!*

A door squeaks, and she drops her washrag. Her heart skips two beats, and she thumps her chest with her fist, wondering how much her body can take in a day. A door squeaks again, and she realizes that she's been hearing the closet door downstairs that Daddy always forgets to spray with WD-40. She laughs. She's been lucky twice. Maybe that's a good sign.

After getting dressed, she climbs downstairs and steps into the kitchen, where breakfast is ready. The breakfast itself is uneventful, with Daddy more interested in the sorry state he thinks the world is in than what Ginny did last night. Ginny helps Mama wash the dishes and finally convinces herself she is off the hook. She turns around, smiles, and looks at Daddy, who smiles back and says, "Ginny, tell us about last night. Weren't you working on algebra with Susie?"

Ginny's heart lurches, and a ball of lead falls into her stomach. Mama turns around and says to Daddy, "Why are you asking her that? You don't trust her?"

Ginny tries to mollify her parents. "It's okay, Mama." Then she turns to Sheldon. "Yes, sir, we were studying for our test today and doing our homework. Algebra homework sure takes a long time to finish. Mrs. Markhard's the worst teacher ever."

Sheldon stands up, and his smile curves into a frown. Ginny remembers the clown in the movie *It*, when Pennywise smiles at a cute little girl. She waves back. The clown's face changes into a horrible scowl. Ginny imagines sharp teeth appearing in Daddy's mouth, the jaw dropping, teeth tearing into her flesh.

Instead of turning into Pennywise, Sheldon glares at Ginny. When he speaks his voice is flat, dispassionate, cold-blooded, like the sharp edge of a hatchet. It cut far more deeply than if he had shouted.

"Algebra class would be a lot easier if you'd really been doing your homework."

Mama's face reddens, and she focuses her eyes on Daddy. Ginny gasps, her head swimming. She struggles to regain control. "What?" she says, trying to sound as incredulous as possible but not, she realizes, doing a good job.

Sheldon moves closer, takes Ginny roughly by the shoulders, and twists her around. He speaks, using the same even voice. "You know what I mean, young lady. Last night, you and that Yankee slut went to a bar and had a shot of bourbon."

Ginny opens her mouth in faux shock. "How... Who... told you this?" she says.

Sheldon speaks through gritted teeth, his flat voice maddening to Ginny. "It doesn't matter who told me. It matters that I know. It matters that you lied to me. It matters that you got drunk."

*Oh God*, Ginny thinks. *Might as well spill the real beans since Daddy's been fed some fake ones.* "I only had one sip from a beer! And I didn't *actually* lie. We really did study after we got back from the bar." Ginny is surprised how lame Susie's suggested explanation sounds when she mouths it herself.

Elma turns around, sighs hard, and walks toward Ginny and Sheldon. "You did lie to us. You know we don't like alcohol, but you drank anyway. You knew you were wrong. You ought to be ashamed of yourself."

Ginny's face burns with mingled shame and fear. Beads of sweat appear on her brow as Daddy points out the error of her ways. "You're underage. Your slutty friend drove while drunk. You two could have killed somebody. You've broken the laws of God and man. I'll report the bar owner later. It all starts with you having one drink. Next you'll have two, then three drinks. It won't stop. You'll be as trashy as that old man down the road with his piles of beer cans and pickled liver. You're a preacher's daughter! Did you even think of what this could do to me? To our entire family? If someone finds out, I could lose my preaching post, and farming by itself won't pay the bills."

"I'm sorry, Daddy," Ginny says. "You, too, Mama. I didn't think of that."

*God, I really am sorry*, Ginny thinks. *Daddy is right; I did wrong, and even though Daddy didn't drink, the rigid Christians who were in his church would fire him in a heartbeat if people found out about what I did. Without the preaching post, he would have to farm full time and try to sell enough crops to make a living – as if that would happen. At least if I had to work for food I wouldn't be a couch potato any more, even though I'd die from exhaustion.*

Sheldon looms over Ginny like a gigantic raven. "You don't think. You feel. And feeling will send you straight to hell. I've cried over your soul. Prayed that God would guide me on how to handle you. So far I've failed you. But I won't fail you again."

Sheldon rears his arm back and strikes Ginny hard across her face with his fist. Ginny swoons and collapses in a heap, and Sheldon pulls back his right arm, the hand balled into a fist. An adrenalin surge energizes Ginny, and she leaps up, red-faced and furious, and charges Sheldon, but he grabs her and shouts, "Go to your room. Now!"

She starts to resist, but thinks better of it. After locking eyes with her father for a moment she lowers her head, says, "Yes Sir," and leaves the room.

Sheldon follows her upstairs and takes a keychain

out of his pocket. "Where did get that?" Ginny asks, gasping. Sheldon says in a voice dripping with sarcasm and spite, "Let's just say that a friend gave it to me. What a privilege it is to carry it."

The allusion to "What a Friend We Have in Jesus" tells Ginny that the monster claiming to be Jesus retrieved her keychain from her purse. Using one arm, Sheldon slings Ginny into her room. Ginny tries to open the door, but he holds the knob tightly. He reaches for a chair and props it under the doorknob.

Ginny screams and pushes the door with all her strength, but it holds fast. She drops onto her hands and knees and peeks underneath the crack at the bottom of the door, seeing only Mama and Daddy's feet.

"You didn't have to hit Ginny so hard," she says. "Using your fist is wrong. You know you could get in bad trouble with the law that way."

Sheldon's lips are hard to distinguish from his red face. He shouts, "Woman, don't tell me what to do with my daughter."

"*Our* daughter," Elma retorts.

Sheldon laughs. "The man has the responsibility for the moral training of children. You only get in the way with your overly soft heart. Women. They're so weak. So pitiful."

Elma points to Sheldon. "I oughta leave you right now," she says. "You've gone plumb crazy on me. If you ever hit Ginny again like that, you'll have hell to pay. Hear?"

Sheldon starts to speak, but Elma silences him with a glare. Sheldon frowns and turns away.

"Ain't you gonna let her get to school?" Elma asks.

"She's already missed the bus."

"Give her an hour," he says. "You can take her to school then."

"All right," Elma says. "Now we need a little talk. You'll do it, too, or else I'll be talking to a lawyer soon."

"I hear you, evil woman," Sheldon says. Elma walks away to the bathroom down the hall. Sheldon storms away from her, his feet pounding the wood floor. The sound of those loud footsteps lessen, and Ginny is alone. Ginny gets up and walks to her bed, where she collapses and starts to cry, in anger as much as hurt. She struggles not to hate Daddy.

She's in her room only a few minutes when she hears footsteps returning, the sound growing louder, then stopping outside her door. Ginny hears a low voice outside her bedroom door. "Now, my beloved daughter," Sheldon says, "spend a little quality time alone. This is for your own good, my dear, to drive you to repentance. Otherwise, you'll roast in hell."

Ginny pulls away from the door and stifles the gagging sound she wanted to make at Sheldon's last three words. *I hate him,* she thinks. *What an exhilarating feeling. I want Daddy to die. He'll lie a coffin, somebody will lower him to the ground, and he'll rot like roadkill. What a thrill. Oh, God, why am I hating? That's one of the worse sins, and it's hurting me. It won't do a thing to stop Daddy. Sweet Jesus, why does hate feel so good?*

Sheldon's footsteps grow softer as he walks away.

Ginny feels totally alone. She paces. She sits. She looks at the clock on the wall. *8:30, and Mrs. Markhard's test is at 10.*

Footsteps approach. There is the sound of

something being dragged away from the door and the doorknob turns. Sheldon's face appears, and Ginny yells, "No!"

Sheldon grins a rictus snarl, then stands aside. "Your mama's gonna drive you to school. You'll be there in plenty of time for your algebra class. Remember what happened, and live accordingly."

"Yes, Sir," is all she says.

# CHAPTER 8

After Ginny's morning, Mrs. Markhard's class was a breeze. Mrs. Markhard took up their homework, avoiding for once making them write their problems on the board, but she passed out a longer, 50-minute test. Ginny thinks she made an A. Susie does not. They are both in the early lunch group, the 11 a.m. group, so they step inside the cafeteria, take their trays of food, and sit by themselves at a table.

"Why aren't you sitting with your boyfriends today?" Ginny asks. "I like to watch the eager looks on their faces before you disappoint them."

"Only most of them," Susie says. "It's too hard to have more than a couple of guys to focus on at once."

"I've changed my mind about having a boyfriend. I think I'd like one, but only one," Ginny says.

Susie examines Ginny's face and asks, "Why are you so late to school? What happened to you? You look like shit."

"Had a fight with Daddy this morning."

"I shouldn't have listened to you," Susie says. "If only I'd been more insistent. I was afraid your father would go batshit. How bad?"

"I can't talk about it."

"Did your dad hit you?"

Ginny wipes away tears. *I'm tired*, she thinks. *Tired of Daddy's emotional abuse, but more tired of figuring out how to feel about him. I hate him and I feel guilty for hating him—then the burn of his palm and the blow of his fist make me hate him again. The false Jesus has poisoned Daddy's mind. There seems no way to get through to him. What if he hits me or Mama hard next time? What if he does even worse?*

"Daddy hit me. He used his fist this time." Ginny says. "He sent me to my room. Even worse, he remembered what that fake Jesus told him."

Susie's face wears an expression of genuine concern. Ginny can't stand fake people, and Susie, despite her popularity with boys and her mischievousness, is for real. Susie asks, "What did your mother do?"

"Mama said that she would leave Daddy if he struck me again. She even used the 'd-word.' Divorce." At the thought of that word new tears gather in Ginny's eyes, but she swipes them away. She sighs. "I think I'm okay. Mama might be okay, even if Daddy gets worse and tries to hurt her. When she was younger she was quite a tomboy. She's 'big-boned,' as we say around here."

"Your dad's a big man, too," Susie says. "He would probably beat her, even if the fight was fair. She might get lucky, I guess. Use a weapon before he knows she has one. But I wouldn't count on it. You need to stay away from there."

Susie's eyebrows furrow as she pauses. Finally she says, "I'm going to call the police. Your father physically abused you. I don't care if it was just one blow. Your face is still a little red."

Ginny waves her arms to dismiss what Susie said. "What would you tell them?" she says. "Most of the sheriff's deputies are dumb as mud. Daddy's known most of the deputies all his life. They have fun listening to him trying to convert them. They'd believe him over us."

Susie sighs and wrings her hands. "But you're hurt! Even redneck deputies would realize they have to do something about that. That welt on your face is physical evidence the deputies cannot deny."

"Daddy's good at making up stories," Ginny says. "He'd say that I fell on the porch and my face hit the hot surface or some other lie. Do you think that Jesus-thing would let Daddy get in trouble with the law? I bet it would stop us if we tried. I wouldn't put it beyond attacking deputies if it thought it could get away with it."

Susie shakes her head. "I don't like this at all. But damn it, I guess you're right. I don't care if your father did remember talking to that thing, that's no excuse for his ratty attitude and behavior. He could have told that thing it's full of shit."

"I know," Ginny says. "I wish he would question things more. Not the big things about God and Jesus. He worries too much over little things. *Drinkin' and dancin,'* he says, *send you straight to Hell."*

Ginny is impressed with her fine imitation of Daddy. Susie laughs.

"You sound just like your father. You could get a job doing imitations. Your father is crazy, and I mean it, girl, to think that you're some kind of 'bad seed.'

You're as much of a goody-goody as I've seen in my life. Your father overreacted big time. Why is he so mad anyway? Because you're underage? That's silly. Most of us at school drink. The bar owner doesn't care, and you hardly had a sip."

"It was still wrong," Ginny says. "We broke the law. You could have hurt us or somebody else driving. My daddy's a preacher, you know. Hare's Corner Church of God Incarnate. To him, dancing and drinking are deadly sins. Lucky for him church members would stay away from that bar. But Daddy and Mama both know I lied to them.

"What's worse, I didn't get a chance to talk to Mama about that Jesus-thing. I'm late because Daddy wedged my bedroom door shut with a chair. He finally let me out. I was amazed he showed some mercy for a change."

Susie lets out a long whistle. "Mercy, my ass. He's up to no good, I tell ya. You've got to get out of there. Your father's religion is making him do worse and worse things to you and your mother. He needs to lighten up big time. I go to church, too. Catholic; couple of times a month. And my mom serves wine with dinner, and we both drink it."

Ginny sighs and shakes her head. "Daddy thinks Catholics aren't really Christians and are all going to hell. I think Mama may be more open-minded."

"Hardcore, girl," Susie says. "What did you do when your father hit you?"

"I wanted to fight, but I knew I stood no chance. Daddy forced me to go to my room." Ginny smiles, shakes her head, and says, "Daddy only hit me because he thinks it will keep me straight, and I'm sure he really thinks Jesus told him to be harder on me."

"That's so fucked up," Susie says.

Ginny reaches over and takes Susie's hand. Ginny says, "Promise me you won't say anything to anyone about this. Please?"

Susie nods and says, "I will if you stay away from that house. We'll figure out something to do. If I had my way, I'd call somebody with authority who's honest; someone other than the sheriff's department. Maybe social services."

Ginny ponders for a moment and says, "Social services has never met an evil Jesus-imposter before. I don't think they'd know what to do. I'll stay with you a while. Will your mother understand?"

Susie replies, "If you don't want her to know about the abuse, I'll have to make up another excuse. Maybe your folks are having problems and they both want you to stay away so they can have some privacy. You'd better hide that red spot on your face where your father hit you. I have some great makeup that'll do the trick."

"I hope that works," Ginny says. "You know that fake Jesus is affecting Daddy. I'm sure the monster comes from that damn barn."

Susie's jaw drops. "Oh my God! You said 'damn.' I told you I'm corrupting you. But you're right about that barn - the freaky light that comes out of it? That scares the hell out of me. And I swear, girl, that paint on the barn looks like fucking blood, especially at night, like it glows. The angles on that barn seem to get weirder all the time. Mother hates that barn, too. She looked over one day and thought she saw a skull's face on the side. She almost ran off the road."

"The barn is evil," Ginny says. "We both saw how Granddaddy hung himself there. For some reason Daddy has tools in there. Why he decided to go inside after his daddy died is a mystery."

"No shit," Susie says.

Ginny says, "Maybe the barn is somehow drawing him in. Like a trap. Or what's behind that Jesus-thing wants to destroy him."

Susie folds her hands tightly across her chest. "You're creeping me out," she says. "Maybe we could hire somebody to burn down the barn. We don't need to be around it at the time."

Ginny shakes her head. "We don't have the money. I'll have to think about what we can do next. I can't hide forever. Daddy will know soon where I'll be staying. If he doesn't already know."

"'Kay, sounds cool to me," Susie says, "but we gotta talk about it soon. What about the dance on Saturday? You were so excited about it."

Ginny lowers her head. "If I went to the dance and Daddy found out, he'd come over to your place and try to get me. He might try to get your mother charged with kidnapping."

"Let him try," Susie says. "Why does he have such a problem with dances?"

"Because he thinks they're evil and lead to fornication - premarital sex. He would do anything if it would save my soul. I don't need to piss Daddy off again. Not with that Jesus-thing telling him what to do. If I go to the dance, it's no telling what Daddy will do. He might hurt me badly; beat me to a pulp, or worse. Even if we went to the dance from your place, that fake Jesus is watching our every move."

"Try not to worry about that now," Susie says. "You have a life to live; your own life, not Sheldon Sprigg's life and certainly not the life of that fake Jesus dude. If you don't go, you're letting that thing win. Com'on! We'll have fun at the dance. YOLO!"

Ginny sighs. "I'll pray it's not the last thing I'll do."

"Relax. We'll kick that thing's ass later. If it has an ass. We can wait until after the dance to figure things out."

"Susie, there's one thing I have to do. We both know Daddy will be mad when 'Jesus' tells him I'm staying with you. If I miss church Sunday he'll go ballistic. I'm going to church Sunday, to both the morning and evening services. If I don't show up there, I don't think Daddy or the fake Jesus will stop until I'm dead. Could you go with me?"

Susie thinks a moment. "Well, it's not our week to attend Mass. I can convince Mom to let me take you myself if she doesn't need the car. I'm worried about you going, though. Your father will take you by force if you refuse to go home. If you're sure about this, I'll go with you."

"I'm sure," Ginny says. "Daddy could take me any time if he wanted to. He hates you and your mom. He thinks you're both bad influences on me, and he wouldn't think twice of rescuing me from your evil clutches."

Susie raises her arms and bends her fingers to look like claws. "My evil clutches," Susie says in a deep voice, and she tousles Ginny's hair with her claws.

Ginny laughs and pushes Susie away. The girls sit in silence, finally eating their lunch.

Two tables behind where Ginny and Susie are

sitting, several students are playing chess. Some students have their trays pushed to the side and are eating as they play. Paul pays little attention to the board and keeps turning around. His opponent moves his queen, and Paul glances back at the board and sighs.

"I resign," Paul says. He shakes hands with his opponent and gets up. He meanders toward the table where Ginny is sitting. He smiles at her, and she smiles back.

"Hi, Paul. Are you going to the school dance?" Ginny's heart pounds, and she fears she has been too bold. Three months of hints failed to get Paul's attention to this point, though the way he looks at her she knows he's interested. Is he interested enough to connect the dots and ask her out?

Paul stumbles over his words. "Uh, thinking about it. You?"

"Yes, I am. Hope to see you there."

"I... I hope to see you there too. Maybe we can dance."

"I'd like that," Ginny says. Paul blushes, waves, and returns to his table as the bell rings. Students pick up their books and book bags and leave the cafeteria.

Susie grins. "Looks like you have some wooin' to do at the dance. He didn't offer to pick you up and make it a date."

Ginny laughs. "He's a nerd. A cute one, but clueless about girls. He'll find out soon enough. I'll make sure of it."

# CHAPTER 9

The next morning, Sheldon steps into the living room and looks around. Elma is holding the phone receiver to her ear. "Why ain't you in the kitchen fixin' breakfast?" Sheldon asks.

"Ginny's not in her room," Elma says. "I've looked everywhere, checked outside, and no sign of her. I've called around, and nobody knows where she is. I tried to call Monica Cottrell. Susie answered the phone and said she's not seen Ginny. Should I call the sheriff?"

"No need to panic," Sheldon says. "She's still mad about her discipline. The sheriff's office won't do anything right way anyway. I'll look for her."

Sheldon walks through the hall, opens the front door to go outside, but a swarm of wasps greets him. He tries to brush them away, but they drive him back inside. He closes the door, and all the wasps stay outside. Sheldon looks out the window and cannot see any wasps, but he dares not open the door. Elma runs through the house to the back door and grabs the knob, but a swarm of wasps reappears out of nowhere. Several wasps land on her hands and sting her. She cries out and releases the door knob. The wasps disappear, as do the welts on her skin.

"Sweet Lord Jesus, what's going on?" Elma asks.

"God is telling us that we are not to contact anyone," Sheldon says. "He will let us know where Ginny is in His own good time."

✦ ✦ ✦

Inside the barn, Satan, back in his true form, rubs his snake-like scales. "Don't rush things, Sheldon," he hisses. "All in good time." His voice changes to Frank Sinatra's and he sings, "I'll do it my way." Satan laughs. "My theme song."

Satan loves the portal in Sheldon's barn. Thousands of years ago, he passed through the portal and entered the world of the Shawnee tribe of Native Americans. But they only hunted in this area, and they avoided the portal as if it were a charging herd of mad bison. Satan figured the portal was a waste of time--until the Scotch-Irish arrived. Their descendants accepted a harsh, legalistic Christianity that Satan liked.

*Once I twist their religion to my liking*, Satan thinks, *I can snag any soul I want. The Spriggs have been good feastings over the years.*

*Sure, I have to put some effort and creativity into it. Sheldon was easy to snag, but not so easy that he became boring like Hollywood actors. Make them lust, their faith goes bust. There are others who make actors seem hard to tempt by comparison: lawyers, journalists, politicians, artists, college professors, and the easiest of all, college administrators. But the Sprigg family, they're refreshing. They require me to use my imagination, and when I finally ensnare a Sprigg, he tastes so good, like a pig roasted on a spit. Time for a good Sprigg pickin'.*

Satan laughs. *Sheldon's legalism is his downfall*, he

thinks. *God, I'm brilliant—you were such a fool to kick me out of Heaven. Now I've created my most brilliant idea yet; to shape-shift into some silly nineteenth century artist's view of Jesus and convince Sheldon that I am Jesus.*

*It was almost too easy, though I softened him up for six months before I finally appeared to Sheldon. The stupid fool forgot that Jesus was a Jew and not the western European in those – ha ha ha - "God-awful" paintings. Sheldon and I will have so much fun in hell. There I won't look like his European Jesus.*

Satan follows the curve of his lip as he traces the perpetually sarcastic smile plastered on it. *First things first. I've set ole' Sheldon on the path to killing Ginny. She'll hate him when she dies, so I'll snatch her soul, too. Sheldon needs a little more persuasion before he gathers the will to kill Ginny, but this man's soul is in the bag.*

"I guarantee it," Satan says, his voice one of some sleazy salesman on a bad TV ad, "or your money back."

✛ ✛ ✛

Later that afternoon Sheldon sits on the living room couch. He grimaces at the sound of dishes rattling and water running in the kitchen. A familiar, honeysuckle sweet voice whispers in his ear, "Sheldon, my child."

Sheldon grins like a toddler with his first toy. "My Lord and Savior!"

The voice continues. "Ginny is at the home of her friends, the idolaters, the ones you call, The Cottrells. She will return, but not here. Search for her on Sunday at church. She will begin her day in your Sunday School class. A splendid opportunity to put the fear of me into her soul. I have some excellent suggestions on how you can do this."

"Yes, Lord. I shall do whatever You want."

Elma walks in and tilts her head as she stares at Sheldon. "Did I hear you talkin' to yourself?"

"No," Sheldon says in a commanding voice. "The voice of Jesus spoke to me, and I know where Ginny is. The Cottrell's."

"Whether he spoke to you or not, that's the most obvious place to hide," Elma replies. "Susie would lie for Ginny, I'm sure. If those wasps let us, we can go there any time. But how do I know you're right, or whether that voice in your head really is Jesus? I can remember when you preached that Jesus didn't speak to folks directly after the time of the apostles. Yet you say He speaks directly to you.

Sheldon clinches his fists. His face reddens. "You dare question my experience?" he asks in an ominous, low tone.

Elma moves closer to Sheldon. "Watch your mouth and unredden that face right now or I'll give it something to be red about."

Sheldon unclinches his fist, though his face remains flushed.

"Even if she's there," Elma says, "she may need a few days to get over what you did to her, you..."

Sheldon pushes his face near Elma's. "I... what?" he says.

Elma backs away and says, "Forget it."

Sheldon speaks in an even voice, his face back to normal. "There is no need to visit Monica Cottrell. Ginny will reappear at church Sunday."

"Jesus tell you that, too?" Elma asks with more than a hint of sarcasm.

Sheldon does not take the bait. "Wait and see," he

says. "I will soon introduce you to Jesus, and you can talk with the Lord face to face like me. Like Moses at the burning bush."

Elma says, "If you're wrong, and she's hurt, you'll be burning inside a bush by the time I get through with you."

Sheldon laughs, a belly laugh that sounds maniacal. Elma freezes, and her body shakes. She clenches her own fists and faces Sheldon. They both stare at one another like boxers before a bout. Sheldon backs away slowly, still laughing, and points at Elma. "Wait and see, foolish woman," he says.

# CHAPTER 10

Susie and Ginny walk into the Morhollow High School gymnasium before the dance begins. Susie wears a low-cut blouse and mini-skirt. Ginny is more modest in a polka-dot dress that still manages to reveal her curves. Susie giggles and points. "Look over there. Paul. I never thought he'd actually show up at a dance. I guess that cafeteria conversation did some good. I've told you how much he eyes you in class."

"Does he really?" Ginny says coyly.

"Yes, he does, girl. Are you blind? Don't you see the way he looks at you when he walks by in the cafeteria? And he's coming this way. I'll leave you two alone. Have fun!" Susie waves at Paul as he passes her. She speaks to him. "Ginny's right over there. She likes you, too."

Paul blushes, then walks over to Ginny and extends his hand awkwardly. He has carrot-top hair that could better be described as orange. Slight and slim, he is only an inch taller than Ginny. He also wears black, thick-rimmed glasses.

*If you look up 'Geek' in the dictionary, Paul's picture would be beside it,* Susie thinks.

When he speaks, his nervous voice shakes as much as his hands. "Hi Ginny! It's good to see you again."

Paul puts his hands in his pockets and shifts around. He looks to the side and doesn't see Ginny's face. Ginny believes he may be slightly autistic, but that's okay with her.

"But I see you in Chemistry every day," she says.

"Yes, but you never talk much other than what we need to do to finish a lab. You're like me in being quiet, I guess. But you seem nice and smart, always making good grades."

Ginny blushes. "I study, that's all. You're the one who's really smart. You make A's without breaking a sweat."

He awkwardly turns his head to look at Ginny directly. "I study, too. Too much, sometimes."

Music begins to play. "Hey, the music's starting," Paul says. "Would... would you... like... to... dance?"

"Yes, Paul," Susie says, breathing out the words.

Paul takes Ginny's hand and they step onto the dance floor. The music's fast at first, and Paul and Ginny look awkward and out of place as they try to club dance. Then the music slows. Paul embraces Ginny, and they close dance. They keep tripping over one another's feet, but they laugh about it and stay locked in a tight embrace.

"I guess we look silly out here," Ginny says.

"Don't think anybody's noticed," Paul says. "Wanna get some air?"

Ginny sighs deeply. "Sure."

They walk outside and stand on the grass next to the full parking lot. They stop and face each other. "Heard you like to read," Paul says.

"As much as I can," says Ginny. "I love *The Lord of the Rings* and the Harry Potter books. I read some Stephen King, too. I hide most of those books from Daddy. He'd burn them if he found them. He's a preacher."

"Sounds like he'd burn my books, too," Paul says. "Edgar Allen Poe. H. P. Lovecraft. Stephen King. Horror stuff. I have a cat skull in my room. Guess I'm weird."

"Not to me," Ginny says, and they embrace.

"I wish I knew what made you tick," Paul says.

Ginny giggles. "I have this heart!"

"I can feel it," Paul says. "So fast." Paul kisses Ginny, at first lightly on the lips, then passionately. They release the kiss and walk back inside, Paul's arm wrapped around her waist. Susie sees them just before the next number starts, smiles, and gives Ginny the thumbs up.

✢ ✢ ✢

As Sheldon walks out the back door, a blue light appears from the area of the barn. As Sheldon approaches the light, the Jesus-figure sits on a tree stump. The Creature raises its hand, and a bright light flashes, striking Sheldon, driving him to his knees.

The Creature thunders as it approaches. "You failed to restrain your daughter. You've failed me. Why haven't you taken her from the evil Cottrell family?"

*Oh Christ, what has she done this time?* Sheldon thinks. *All the work I put into that girl; I've worked my heart out to raise a good child, and she disappoints again and again. Now I have to deal with Jesus' wrath.*

Sheldon coughs out an answer. "You said she'd be at church. I thought I would make her go home then.

That seemed to be what you wanted, Lord." Sheldon shivers, hearing too late the tinge of sarcasm in his voice.

"Don't question me in that tone of voice, you fool," the false Jesus says. "I can crush you into the dust from whence you came any time I desire. You have eyes, yet you do not see. Ginny took advantage of her freedom. She was at the dance tonight, being fondled by a boy."

Sheldon thinks, *Shit,* and is grateful that the word didn't slip. He is afraid Jesus read his mind since Christ knows all, but Jesus does not react. Sheldon puts his head into his hands. "Oh God, no," he says.

The imposter grabs Sheldon by the neck as if he were scruffing a cat. "You stupid fool," he says. "Don't you know Ginny always takes advantage of a lack of supervision. Ginny's little friend Susie drove her to the dance. The evil pagan. Worshiping my mother as if she were a goddess. Changing the truth of God into a lie."

"Oh, Jesus," says Sheldon.

"If that was a prayer, I have an answer," says the Beast. "A difficult one. Ginny will soon be beyond redemption. But it's not too late. If she were to be sacrificed now, I would forgive her transgressions. But for her to abide with me forever, you must now do what's best for her soul."

Sheldon's heart lurches with a surge of fear. He wonders what Jesus meant, and suddenly he recalls the story of God commanding Abraham to sacrifice his son Isaac. *Not that, Lord*, Sheldon thinks. *God spared Isaac, but Isaac had not sinned grievously. Ginny obviously has.*

Heart racing like a revving engine, Sheldon asks, "Lord?"

The Lord of this World pinches Sheldon's cheeks like a mother scolding a naughty child and says, "Have you no ears to hear? I see Ginny's future. Soon nothing will halt her course of disobedience. Unless she is no longer in a position to disobey. There's only one way to guarantee that."

Sheldon shakes his head as if in a daze. *He does want me to kill her*, he thinks. *Oh Jesus, no, not that, please.*

"Lord, I cannot," he says.

"Obey me," says the demonic false Jesus in a voice so loud the ground shakes underneath him. "You know what must be done. Fail to save her and I will torture you both forever in hell. If Elma gets in the way, remember, she is keeping Ginny's immortal soul hostage. She would allow Ginny to burn forever in sulfur fire. That's worse than any kind of death this side of hell. If you do not obey I will keep all of you separated from each other for eternity. Now go before I change my mind."

Sheldon runs, holding his hands to his face. He stumbles in the dark and falls down. The soft glow from the light by the false Christ fades, and it is pitch black except for the window at the back door. Sheldon crawls up the steps and lets himself inside. He stumbles to the foot of the stairs and sobs.

# CHAPTER 11

In the barn the Beast laughs. *The Beast* is his favorite name, one of so many his admirers and detractors have given him over the years. He appreciates the scene in the original *Poltergeist* movie in which the short medium with the annoying little girl voice tells the haunted family that the entity talking to their daughter with a child's voice is... *The Beast*. She said those words with a throaty whisper that made Satan seem so creepy.

Satan laughs. *I am creepy,* he thinks, and he scratches his face with his claws, tearing off clods of skin and bloody muscle. He says to himself with another maniacal laugh, "Don't worry about it son, it'll grow back."

*Dear old Sheldon. I so love to mess with his mind, to use the American expression. I tell Sheldon to do one thing: Let Ginny stay at the Cottrells. Then I stop Sheldon and Elma from traveling to the Cottrells or calling the sheriff. Stinging insects always come in handy. Then I condemn Sheldon for doing what I'd told him to do in the first place. I am so brilliant! And Sheldon, the poor bastard, is so confused. I'll enjoy the memory of Sheldon's lost look for a long, long time.*

✦ ✦ ✦

Ginny tosses and turns. A night light by her bed goes black, and the room turns dark as a sunless cave. A gray light permeates the room. Ginny sits up, gasping. A light shaft appears and forms the shape of a door in front of her. She rises from her bed and walks into the light.

Ginny finds herself standing on top of a craggy hill. In the distance she sees an ancient city, Jerusalem, and in its center, sitting atop a hill, is the shining Temple of Herod, just like the pictures she's seen in the family Bible. Ginny starts. A man is walking towards her, shimmering in the Near Eastern summer sun. He appears to be Jesus. Ginny falls on her knees, extends her arms toward the figure and says, "My Savior!"

*Jesus* extends his hand, and Ginny is about to take it, touch it with her fingertips. Suddenly Jesus turns into Sheldon. A demon, smiling with thick, red lips, appears beside Sheldon. It opens its mouth unnaturally wide and swallows Sheldon whole.

Ginny springs up in her bed, stifling a scream. She wills her panting breaths to slow, her thudding heart to calm. She looks around the room, tries to get her bearings, and remembers that she's in a guest bedroom at Susie's house. She sighs, and whispers, "Thank you Jesus. Just a dream."

The next morning Susie slides the sports car into the parking lot of the Hare's Corner Church of God Incarnate. Old people leaving their cars glare as the car spins to a halt in the gravel, stirring up a huge pile of white dust. Susie and Ginny get out of the car and march toward the house-like wood building with its attractive, covered front porch and two pews bordering the doors. They walk through the auditorium toward the back, to stares from members, and open one of the doors behind the pulpit to the Sunday School rooms. Ginny points out the right room and they step inside and sit beside each other around a rectangular table. Sheldon enters the room, a regal figure wearing a dark blue suit and matching tie. Susie glares at him the entire class. He begins his lesson.

"Today, young people, I want to talk to you about what happens to those who disobey God. About hell. I want you to imagine the hottest day you've experienced. Suddenly you start to float. You float above the clouds, above the air. Your body is protected by some kind of life support field, but it does not protect you from the sun's heat. Soon, to your horror, you realize you are flying toward the sun. You pass Venus. By then your skin starts to boil, and burns cover your body. Blisters burst and re-form and your skin heals and burns again. You pass Mercury. The light burns into your eyes which are unable to close — but the light does not put out your eyes. They hurt more and more with the light and the heat. You're inside the corona, then on the sun's surface. No hope. You're pulled, pulled, pulled by something into the center of the sun. Your flesh burns through, but your nerves miraculously remain, and you feel the pain of a fire over a million degrees hot. As your flesh repairs itself, you feel every burned part itch, but won't be able to scratch. One you're fully healed, you boil again. Your agony only gets worse with time. That pain you feel is nothing compared to the pain of an eternity in hell."

The students squirm. Some have tears in their eyes; others appear eager to hear more. Sheldon looks Ginny straight in the eye, his face red. He continues, "Some of you may lie, even to your parents. Some of you may have attended the dance last night. Christ sees all. And Jesus will not tolerate disobedience. Is hell the fate you want?"

Sheldon's face changes, his teeth seem to disappear, and his grin is pure sarcastic spite. Rob, a high school football player, moans, "Ohhhhh," as if he were in pain. Two girls sit frozen in their seats. One boy punches the boy next to him and says, "Did you see what I just saw?" The other boy nods, his eyes wide. Ginny starts to shake, then she cries out and runs out the door, closely followed by Susie. Students start talking, but Sheldon silences them. "Quiet! Class is dismissed."

Despite her trauma and over Susie's objections, Ginny insists on attending the main service and sitting in her usual pew. Susie joins her, and they sit on a pew near the front of the church. Ginny wipes tears from her eyes. Elma sits beside her, trying to comfort her. Susie sits on the other side. She fixes her eyes on Sheldon again, her face twisted in hate. Elma speaks to Ginny in a low voice. "I'm so glad you came. What's wrong, honey?"

Ginny shakes her head and takes another tissue out of her purse. She looks at Elma and smiles.

"Nothing, really," she says. "Just girl stuff."

Elma pats Ginny on the shoulder. Sheldon walks to the pulpit, ready to present his sermon. Some of the teens in the audience lower their heads and shut their eyes. Sheldon scans the audience without saying a word. People start fidgeting in their seats. He continues to look around for a couple of minutes, then speaks in a low, calm voice.

"Christ has made clear to me, and to you, the penalty of hell for those who disobey. We must do what is best for our souls." Sheldon raises his voice. "Last night there was a dance at the high school, inflaming students' lust. They will pay for their sins." Sheldon looks Ginny in the eye.

She gasps, whispers to Susie, "Oh, God, he knows."

"The bastard," Susie says, and an old woman in front of her turns around and stares at Susie with a sour look that makes her face look like a dried prune. Susie smiles at her. The woman rubs her ears as if wondering if she heard what she thought she heard.

Sheldon continues, raising his voice. "And there are those who lead astray the faithful. Alcoholic, fornicating Papists, for instance. They may sneak in to spy on God's people and keep their prey at bay. They will pay soon. Very soon."

"Mother fuc..." Ginny grabs Susie's arm and shakes her head.

"No, Susie," she whispers. "That will only egg him on." Sheldon keeps upping the vitriol, and Susie's face reddens to the color of a ripe tomato, but they manage to survive the rest of the sermon and the service. Ginny struggles to keep control of herself and to keep control of Susie. She fears what Susie might say to Daddy. And what Daddy's response would be.

# CHAPTER 12

Ginny goes home with her parents. If she had fought them there, it would have been two against two, but she is convinced the Jesus-figure would come to help Sheldon. Someone, perhaps her, perhaps Susie, perhaps Mama, would get hurt. Now she lies on her bed, crying. Sheldon knocks on her door, then enters. Ginny sees no choice but to grovel.

"I'm sorry, Daddy," she says in her most pitiful voice. "I won't go to any dance again."

"I don't believe you," Sheldon says. "Twice now you've shown me you can't be trusted. There are no more chances for you."

Ginny does not like the sound of that and asks, "Are you going to hit me again? It's not right for you to hit me."

"I have a right to do far more than that," Sheldon says, and Ginny feels deathly afraid.

Sheldon loses all control. "Harlot!" he screams with a shrill sound that seems out of place coming from such a big man. "You dare tell me right from wrong! Jesus decides that for me. Your mama is not here to spoil you today. I never told her about your lie. Now you've run away without letting us know where you were. But we're by ourselves, now, aren't we, my disobedient daughter?"

Ginny stops caring what will happen to her. If Daddy insists on being so stupid, she will show him up. She yells at the top of her voice, "Disobedient? To *your* Jesus, maybe. Not to *mine*."

Sheldon raises his hand, and Ginny sees the glint of a knife. He swings it toward her chest but she is ready and slides to the side, the knife missing her and digging into the wood in the wall. As Sheldon struggles to pull out the knife, Ginny darts through the door and gets away. Outside she finds her old bicycle and pedals down the driveway toward Allenville Road. Sheldon runs after her about a football field's length, stabbing the air. He stops and kneels down, panting with exhaustion.

*I may be a couch potato*, Ginny thinks, *but at least I am a young couch potato.*

Ginny flees toward the Cottrell house, constantly checking behind her for Sheldon's car. She reaches the house and bangs on the door with her fists. Monica answers. "My God, Ginny! Are you all right?"

Ginny forces herself to stand still. Her jackrabbit heart slows enough for her to answer, "Sorry... out of breath..."

"Something has to be wrong. Are you still having problems with your parents? Did one of them try to hurt you? You look like you're scared half to death."

"Stuff's still going on. But I can't..." Ginny pauses, takes some deep breaths. "I can't talk about it now."

"Okay, but if you're in big trouble or are in danger

in any way, let us know, please."

"Of course I will."

"Maybe some ginger cookies would help you feel better. I just baked some."

"Thank you, Mrs. Cottrell. I'll have some cookies… and some water to drink, if you don't mind. Is Susie here?"

"She's in her bedroom listening to music on her computer. Ginny, how many times must I tell you to call me Monica? I'll bring you a pitcher of water and a glass when I bring the cookies."

Ginny steps inside. "Thanks, Monica." She walks toward Susie's bedroom, knocks, and opens the door. Susie gets up, hugs her, and says, "I knew you'd be back. You're in too much danger at your house. But God! You're out of breath."

"A hard, fast bike ride," Ginny says. "You've probably guessed that Daddy found out about me being at the dance," Ginny says. "He tried to stab me…"

"Stab you?" Susie says. "Call the cops. Don't be a fool. I'm glad you got away, but how long do you figure you can stay lucky? You can't be around your father, at least as long as he's going ape-shit. Call the authorities now. If he's crazy, then he'll get medical care. There's no rule that says he has to go to jail."

"I would call if only I were involved," Ginny says. "But Mama's in danger, too. If Daddy would stab me, he'd kill Mama for sure, especially if he thought she called the cops instead of me."

"Not if they took him to jail," Susie says.

"I can't take the risk that he'll talk his way out of that," Ginny says.

"Well, hell," Susie says. "I wonder why your father

has not driven by to get you. He's bound to know where you've gone."

Ginny shivers. "I'm sure he knows. If not, that Jesus-thing will tell him. How can we stop something that knows everything we do?"

Susie takes a hard, deep breath and says, "Thinking is so hard. With the cops out of the picture for now, why not tell your mother everything? We've talked about this before, remember? You said she is more open-minded than your father. She might listen. Have you tried to tell her anything yet?"

Ginny wrings her hands. "Every time I try Daddy gets in the way. He knows too much. I hate staying there, but I don't want Daddy to hurt Mama. He's so crazy it's no telling how far he'd go. I think we should bring Paul into this. He's into ghosts and monsters. I think he'll believe us. He may know something we can do."

Susie smiles. "Great idea. Call him, and we'll catch him up."

"After that," Ginny says, "we'll find a back way to get to my house. I'm afraid that thing told Daddy to kill me. That would explain the knife lunge. Since Daddy thinks this monster is really Jesus, he'd do anything to make sure I'm dead the next time he attacks. I'll stay here tonight and pray Daddy doesn't drop by."

Ginny phones Paul and explains the situation. "Wow, that's cool," he says.

"You believe me?" Ginny asks.

"Of course. I've done ghost investigations before and seen weirder things. I think we ought to burn down the barn. It's an evil place. If we can't do that, we can investigate inside the barn. I know that's scary since that vision you told me about, but the evil has to be stopped before you are hurt—or worse."

After hanging up, Ginny updates Susie.

"Won't your parents be looking for you tomorrow?" Susie asks.

"They'll know I'm safe here," Ginny says, "and if Daddy didn't have to do farm work he'd be on the lookout. But all day tomorrow he has to sow soybeans while it's sunny. After that there's a chance of rain the rest of the week. Mama will be busy on her shopping day with her friends in Nashville. I'm betting she'll go as long as she figures I'm safe."

The following afternoon, Susie, Paul, and Ginny gather bags of supplies, including flashlights, matches, and Paul's equipment he uses for "ghost hunting," including a thermometer, camera, and electromagnetic field detector. They sit in a pocket in a patch of tall hay near the Sprigg house. Ginny tells Paul, "It's a good thing that your dad had that extra can of gas in the shed. Now we can get rid of that barn for good."

Susie frowns. "Are you sure your parents won't see us if one of them gets back early?"

"We'll stay low, that's for sure. Somehow I feel like that Jesus-thing is holding back. I wish I knew the reason."

"I'm not complaining about that," Susie says.

The group sneaks into the back yard, where they hide behind honeysuckle bushes. The hum of the planter in the field mixes with the sound of a loud mockingbird at the top of an oak tree. Ginny, Susie and Paul crouch down and sneak to the side of the barn opposite the house. There they squat, and Paul splashes gasoline on the side of the barn. He places newspapers on the ground next to the barn and pours gasoline on them. Next to the gasoline-filled paper he places two dry newspapers.

"Okay, Ginny," Paul says. "Go ahead and light the edge of the paper."

"Remember the plan," Ginny says. "We run into the woods, hide behind bushes, and watch."

Ginny lights the paper, and the group quickly slips through a gap in the fence into the woods. The fire spreads to the gasoline-soaked paper, and it explodes into bright flames that lick the side of the barn. A few seconds later, the flames go out.

"What the hell?" Susie says. "The fire went out. It's not, like, even a minute yet. Shit like that can't be happening."

Ginny is not surprised, but her stomach still sinks with disappointment. *Lord, please give us a break*, she thinks. A twinge of guilt tightens her stomach into a knot, so she prays silently, *Lord, forgive me for getting impatient with you.* Out loud she says, "Let's get back to the barn."

They return to the barn and find it has not been harmed by the fire. There is no effect on the barn's blood-red color. Susie wrings her hands. "It won't burn. You have any other bright ideas, Paul?"

"Hey!" Ginny says. "You went along with it, too."

Paul smiles and takes Ginny's hand. Ginny doesn't appreciate Susie's attitude, but she understands her frustration level. It makes sense that the barn had been a source of evil since it had been built, given its eerie preservation over the years. She doubts that they are the only ones who recognized the barn's evil and tried to destroy it with fire or in some other way. Yet they had to try, and Paul recognized that.

*We're not trying to punch ourselves out of a paper bag,* Ginny thinks, her hope level at the point of crashing. *We're trying to punch out of a reinforced steel room.*

Susie says, "Sorry, Gin, but Paul is supposed to be the expert on this stuff, and if his best idea doesn't work, we're screwed. Aren't there groups that know what they're doing? Maybe we should call somebody from one of those ghost hunting groups?"

"I doubt we're dealing with a ghost," Paul says. "Most of those groups don't know what they're doing, anyway. I'll take a temperature reading here and then one in the barn. If there is some kind of demon or spirit inside the barn, there might be a cold spot where the temperature is much cooler. We need to get inside that barn to the source of the fake Jesus's power. Both of you say there is a hole in there. I bet that's where we need to focus."

"Oh, great," Susie says. "I'm not going inside that barn again. I'm afraid I wouldn't make it out alive."

Ginny's heart lurches with a rush of adrenalin. "Are you sure we have to get back inside that evil place?"

"Not totally," Paul admits. "I'm afraid if you don't stop it, whatever it is, it might follow you. Then leaving the house and barn would be no protection. Whatever it is making your daddy nuts is getting stronger. You noticed those flames didn't affect the barn at all. If a power can protect 100-year-old wood from burning, I'm afraid to think what else it can do."

"Could it be the paint?" Susie asks. "Maybe we can try scraping it off."

"It's worth a shot," Paul says. Ginny runs to the

shed and finds some rough sandpaper. She rubs it against the barn, but it has no effect. Paul tries, and then the three of them push and pull the sandpaper back and forth across the paint at the bottom. Nothing happens. There is no trace of paint on the sandpaper.

"Damn it," Susie says.

"You came up with a great idea," Paul said. "We had to try. There's some power maintaining that barn. As long as the power is present, we can forget about destroying the barn. Even if we could destroy the barn, what would we do about the hole? Fill it up? Somehow I think that would be a dead end, too."

Ginny squeezes Paul's hand and says, "I'm scared half to death. But I trust you. It looks like the only remaining option is going inside the barn. Let's do it. Susie, are you with us?"

Susie sighs loudly. "Yeah, I guess so. If I die, my ghost will haunt my lawyer into suing your asses off. Well, get inside already."

Susie picks the lock again, and Ginny lifts the lever and cracks the door. Susie pulls out her iPhone, hits the flashlight app and gives it to Ginny. Out of habit, Ginny tries the light switch, but it doesn't work. She leads the group, followed closely by Paul, then Susie. "Shut the door, Susie," Ginny says. "I know it's scarier with the door shut to the outside, but Daddy doesn't need to know we're in here."

Susie closes the door behind her. "Damn, it's cold in here!" Susie says, and she huddles close to Ginny.

"Hand me the thermometer I put in the bag," Paul says.

Ginny reaches inside, finds the thermometer, and gives it to Paul. He takes it, a digital maximum-minimum thermometer, and sets it on the barn floor.

"Temperature dropping," Paul says. "70... 65... 60... 55... holding steady at 48. That's a 30-degree difference. It was 78 outside when I checked."

Susie asks, "Isn't a drop in temperature a sign of a ghost?"

"Not necessarily," Paul replies, "but it's certainly is a sign of something paranormal. And I bet it's something bad. Hey, what's that?"

There is a strong breeze that tousles the teens' hair. Ginny lets the beam from the iPhone flashlight scan the barn's interior. She hands the device back to Susie when Paul pulls out a large LED he uses on ghost investigations from his bag. The LED illuminates most of the interior, but casts eerie shadows against the barn walls. There is no sign of anything amiss, other than the breeze. There is a clear view of the abyss in the barn floor.

"It's getting colder," Paul says. He rechecks the thermometer. "Down to 40 degrees. The source of this wind must be...of course!" Paul points. "From the hole in the floor."

The breeze grows stronger, driving the group back.

"I think we need to back off now," Ginny says, and they run toward the barn door, which opens before they get there. A dark figure bars the way and looms over them like a bird of prey. He seizes Susie by the shirt. Paul shines his light at the figure. It is Sheldon Sprigg. The brilliant light from the LED lantern should have blinded him, at least momentarily, but it has no effect. Sheldon moves forward, carrying a squirming and cursing Susie. His left arm latches around her throat and his right hand seals her mouth.

His voice booms out, "How dare you trespass!"

Paul stands back, horrified and impotent. Sheldon takes his hand off Susie's mouth. He repositions himself so that both his hands are wrapped around Susie's throat.

Susie's voice is a harsh whisper. "Let me go! I'll have your ass in jail for assault."

To everyone's surprise, Sheldon releases Susie, and she falls back, gagging. Sheldon claws for Ginny. She pulls away, but his hands grasp her blouse, tearing it, exposing her bra. Sheldon stops and stares, his mouth open. Then he swallows hard, his eyes still focusing on Ginny's body.

Ginny begins to cry, and she runs into Paul's arms. She feels she never really knew her daddy. Nausea overwhelms her, and she tells Paul, "Could you lower me to the floor. I need to sit down." Paul eases her to the floor and sits beside her. "You pervert!" she shouts at Sheldon. "The way you looked at me with lust. Your own daughter. This is who you really are! Oh, God, the evil was already inside you! That fake Jesus you think is real may be a monster or some kind of demon, but it has a lot to work with, doesn't it, Daddy?" Ginny spits out the "D" on "Daddy." Ginny wants her sarcasm to be so palpable that Sheldon can taste the sourness in the air.

Sheldon clinches his fists, and his voice turns low and ominous. "You ungrateful bitch! It is Jesus who talks to me! My Lord and Savior, whom you, rebellious slut, disobey. I try to keep you from hell, and you bring your pagan, Mary-worshipping friend and that piece of marshmallow you call a *boyfriend*. As for the rest of you... Ginny's my daughter, and this is my property you're standing on. I'll call the law on all you spoiled brats. You are the real demons, spewing disobedience like vomit."

Ginny and Paul stand up, but Sheldon moves over to Paul and pulls him up and away from Ginny. Ginny struggles, and Sheldon pushes her to the ground. Paul swings his fists at Sheldon, but he misses. Sheldon slams Paul against the barn door and grabs his throat. Ginny stretches her fingers and scratches Sheldon with her nails. Sheldon jerks back, stumbles and falls. He regains his feet, then points at Paul.

"I'll deal with my spoiled daughter later," he says. "As for you, boy, if I see you again around my daughter, you will have permanent damage to your ability to have children. Now, git!"

Susie puts her arm around Ginny's shoulder. Paul runs to Ginny and wraps his arm around her other shoulder. He looks at Sheldon and smiles widely.

Sheldon's face turns so red and wrinkled it resembles the face of a mad clown. He runs toward them and shouts near Paul's ear, "What did I just tell you, boy?"

The wind grows louder, then stops. The air is still, the barn silent. Dread seeps into Ginny, and she can't shake the feeling of the presence of pure evil. Something rises from the hole in the floor. Ginny quickly shines her light on the figure. It looks like Jesus rising as if from a grave. Ginny thinks if this were the real Jesus the effect would be awe-inspiring, but all she feels is terror boiling her blood.

Sheldon, ever the true believer, rushes toward the hole and kneels, bowing his head to the ground. The false Jesus raises Sheldon and flies toward the door with him, planting Sheldon square in front of the barn door, blocking the way out.

"Don't let them out," the false Jesus commands. Then the creature floats in the air and sinks down onto the floor, where he faces the teens. Paul stands up and takes Ginny and Susie's hands, turning them around to face the door, but the creature pushes them away with arms that stretch snakelike, beyond their normal length. Sheldon trudges toward the teens, his arms extended like some Frankenstein monster. Ginny, Paul, and Susie are trapped.

Thoughts flicker through Ginny's mind. *The Jesus-thing has taken a bodily form. If that body can feel pain, perhaps I can hurt him.*

Ginny rears her head and lowers it toward the creature. Her teeth clamp down, and the creature flinches just enough for her to escape. She hits the fake Jesus with a left hook followed by a hard right. The beast's body begins flickering back to its demon-form.

Ginny screams. "Daddy, look at what you're worshipping," she shouts, but Sheldon is now fully focused on attacking Paul. The demonic figure, shaken out of its false form by Ginny's resistance, clearly wishes to avoid Sheldon seeing him as he really is. The demonic figure rises into the air over the heads of the others in the barn and flies, head-first, into the hole in the floor as Susie and Paul watch, frozen, unable to reach Sheldon in time to make him see the true nature of what he's been trusting and obeying.

Paul and Ginny rush out the door with Sheldon following close behind. Just before Susie can escape, Sheldon grabs her arm, and the barn doors, seemingly on their own, slam shut, trapping her arm. She screams, and the door gives way enough for Sheldon to pull her inside. "Help!" she says. "He's got me."

Ginny turns around and shouts, "Daddy, stop!" She turns to Paul and says, "Stop him. He'll kill her."

Ginny takes one side of the barn door and Paul takes the other. They barely get their fingers inside the groove as Susie's screams grow louder, followed by a brief silence before Sheldon's voice booms out. "Bitch! You bit me! I'll kill you, you little whore!"

"God. Please help us," Ginny says. She and Paul pull harder, and the door gives way enough for Paul to push his hand inside. He grabs Susie's hand and pulls hard. Susie pops out, stumbling. Paul and Ginny help her up.

Sheldon pushes the barn door open, but before he can run outside Ginny kicks him in the groin. He collapses, rolling and moaning on the ground, but the demon reappears in his Jesus form. He does not follow them but remains beside Sheldon.

The teens run toward the house and stop behind a wood storage shed. Susie collapses, holds her stomach, and retches.

Sheldon regains his feet and stumbles after them, his hands clenched into fists. The Jesus-figure shambles along behind him. Ginny drags Susie to her feet. "Run!" Paul yells.

They pass the boundaries of the back yard into the cornfield. Ginny's mind races, thinking of all the ways she imagined she would die. Being killed by her own father and a demonic fake Jesus was never one of them.

She girds up her courage. *It's not going to happen*, she thinks. *We're going to live through this.* The Beast reaches for Paul and grabs him on the shoulder. Paul screams as steam rises from the spot the Beast's claws touched. Paul jerks away and runs, but Sheldon is catching up. Ginny prays silently. With a final effort, Paul and the group put some distance between themselves and Sheldon, and they run in a zig-zag pattern between the corn stalks.

They reach the border of the woods, where an old fence marks the boundary. Ginny looks behind her and feels faint as the demonic false Jesus and Sheldon begin to float toward her and her friends. They reach the teens and sink to the ground. Sheldon snatches Susie and grips her throat. She gags and passes out. Ginny screams and rushes at Sheldon. His arms unfurl from around Susie's neck, and his fist slams into Ginny's jaw. She falls unconscious. The Jesus-figure touches Paul with two hands on his head, and he screams again. His hair is singed and smoking, but he manages to keep struggling. He takes a deep breath, and speaks. "In the name of the real Jesus, demon, show yourself."

The Jesus figure flickers and suddenly flies away, rising into the sky, floating toward the barn. Its demonic form begins to reassert itself as it floats out of visual range behind a tree. Paul picks up a large limestone rock from the ground and strikes Sheldon on the head, knocking him unconscious. Ginny starts to wake up. Paul takes her hand, kisses her on the forehead, and asks, "Are you okay?"

Ginny rubs her jaw. "I think so. Oh Paul, what happened to your hair? Your shoulder is burned, too." She looks to the side and says, "Oh. God. Susie."

Ginny and Paul run to Susie. Ginny moves close to Susie's face, stays there for a moment, then raises her head and says, "I feel her breathing."

Susie stirs, moves her head to face the side where Sheldon lies. Susie cringes and cries out when she sees Sheldon. She tries to get up, but Ginny gently shoves her down. "Don't move yet. We don't know how bad you're hurt."

Susie's words come haltingly. "Your...dad, Ginny. He's...still breathing. Kill him while you have a chance."

"I can't kill my own daddy, no matter how bad he is," Ginny says.

Susie speaks again, more in control of her voice. "But he tried to kill you. Tried to kill us all. He'll do it, too, if we don't stop him. What do you have to say about this, Paul?"

"I want to kill Mr. Sprigg. Or at least I'm mad enough to. But I agree with Ginny for different reasons. Whatever possessed Mr. Sprigg might move into someone else once he is dead; you, your mama, Ginny, or me. Maybe someone else. We may not be as strong as Sheldon, but that thing, that demon or whatever it is, makes whomever it possesses have superhuman strength. It could make us strong enough, and mean enough, to hurt someone badly. Hopefully not strong enough to kill."

Before they can stop her, Susie sits up. She says, "You guys. Why do you have to be so damned logical, Paul? Can't we tie Mr. Sprigg up?"

"There's rope in the storage shed," Ginny says," "but we're exhausted and that's a long way to walk. Daddy would probably wake up before we have a chance to tie him up."

"Do you think he'll try to hurt your mother?" Paul asks.

"Definitely. He may not try right away, though,"

Ginny says. "He'll recuperate, then talk with that false Jesus who will tell Daddy his next move."

Paul stands, looks around, and says, "I think we should get some distance between us and Mr. Sprigg. Let's cross the fence into the woods. That's Herbert Miller's property."

"Does he shoot trespassers?" Susie asks.

Paul laughs. "Goodness, no. He's not a fan of people hunting on his property without permission, but he told me that as long as it's not hunting season I could walk on his land. He's old and knows a lot about the history of this area. He may know more about the history of the barn and Ginny's ancestors."

"His house is close by, about a half mile from here," Ginny says. "I've stopped by there before because he's let me eat watermelon, and he always gives me a Popsicle in the summer.

"Yolo, guys. We'd better leave. Ginny's father is starting to stir. Should I conk him on the head again?"

"No," Ginny says. "That might kill him. Let's go."

Paul squirms under the fence and helps Susie get through. Ginny finds a low spot in the fence nearby and climbs to the top, falling with a hard *thud* to the ground. She laughs and joins the others, who work their way about 100 yards into the woods. They hide behind some bushes and watch Sheldon, who stirs and rubs his head. He turns toward the barn and starts walking.

"There he goes," Susie whispers.

"Like a dog returning to his vomit," Ginny says.

"Eww," Susie says. "You don't have to be gross."

The group continues their walk, moving between bushes and dodging briers along the way. Suddenly a shadow looms over them. They freeze. They hear a loud voice.

# CHAPTER 13

W hat are you kids doin' in my woods?"

They turn and come face to face with an old man with an etched face and gray hair, dressed in a farmer's overalls. He looks at Paul and says, "Come on, boy, I know you. Figured I'd joke around with you and give you a little scare." Herbert Miller tousles Paul's hair and starts to laugh. Susie pouts and speaks.

"Dude, if you knew what happened to us you wouldn't scare us out of half our lives. You've got to be Mr. Miller."

Herbert looks them over and says, "That's right. I'm Herbert Miller. You children look like you've seen the old devil himself."

He motions them over to a clear area in the shade. Ginny scans the woods that seem so ordinary in the daylight. Sycamores, oaks and lots of cedars. Moss growing through cracks in limestone rocks. Wildflowers that seem to sprout everywhere, clumps of bluebells, and yellow and white flowers she can't identify. The dappled beauty of sunlight and shade. The cool breeze wafting through the trees into the clearing. How horror itself could thrive less than a mile from such beauty is something she cannot understand.

*Why did God allow a mockery of Jesus to hurt Daddy? Maybe I was right when I told Daddy that he already had deep evil within himself. I'm so scared! For Mama, for Susie, for Paul—and for me.*

She tries to be compassionate toward Daddy. After all, no person is without fault.

*Any of us,* she thinks, *could have fallen to that Beast if it caught us off guard. Only grace can get us through this.*

*But that's what that thing wants. It wants Daddy to murder me and it wants me and everyone else to hate Daddy. If I have to kill him to protect Paul and Ginny, I will. I don't know if I can do it without hating him, though. That's the rub. What if by killing the possessed, I become possessed? And then.... Lord, I don't want to think about that.*

Her mind shuts out the grim thoughts, and she focuses her attention on Herbert Miller.

Herbert motions the group to a long log, and the teens sit there. Herbert sits on a stump on the other side. "I was trimmin' some bushes close to the woods when I heard some commotion," he says. "When I got close enough I recognized your voices, Paul and Ginny. You," he says, pointing to Susie, "I ain't familiar with."

"I'm Susie Cottrell." Susie switches to a fake Southern accent. "I ain't from around these here parts."

"Susie," Ginny scolds.

But Herbert laughs, "I see you ain't. New York City, I'd guess. Oh, don't look at me like I've never been anywhere in my life. I've seen New York. Used to visit there from time to time with an old folks traveling group at church. I think you're from, yeah, Brooklyn."

Susie smiles. "I'm impressed, Mr. Miller. I'm sorry for being such a smart as... I mean, smart-aleck."

"Don't be silly," Herbert says. "I've seen Yankee smart mouthed people and Southern ones. I reckon I prefer the Yankees because I expect them to be that way. Southern folks who are smart-alecks ain't raised right."

Ginny looks at Susie, who appears a little miffed at Mr. Miller's prejudice against people from the north. *She'll get over it.*

"What happened to you three?" Herbert asks.

Ginny, Susie and Paul look at one another. Finally, Ginny speaks. "You won't believe us. It's too weird."

"You might be surprised what I'd believe," Herbert says. "Why don't you take a deep breath and start talkin'. I'll listen, and I promise I won't make fun of you, no matter how strange you think your tale is."

Ginny takes that deep breath and says, "Daddy and a demon tried to kill us! We barely got away! I know; you think we're nuts."

Mr. Miller looks at Ginny, all traces of a smile gone from his face. His hands start to shake. "You're not nuts. I have a feeling you folks are some of the sanest people around her. Go on and tell the rest."

Ginny notices Mr. Miller's reaction and feel a flash of new fear, and her heart skips a beat. She swallows, and focuses on staying calm enough to explain what happened from the start. *He must know something about what's happening. Maybe he has a way he can help us. I have to get this out without freaking.* Ginny takes another deep breath, closes her eyes, and says, "It started with Daddy acting strange. Then he met this *thing* that looked like Jesus. Daddy started hitting me, saying I was a rebellious child for going to the dance and for, uh, well, I had one sip of beer at a bar."

Herbert smiles. "Ah, an underage drinker," he says. He turns to Susie and says, "I suspect you put her up to it."

Susie glares at Herbert and opens her mouth to speak, but he laughs and continues talking. "Don't worry, young lady. You did wrong, but we have a lot more to worry about now. I warned Sheldon, but he never listened. Stubborn as a mule like his daddy. Elma knew *some* things, but not the whole story. She figured since they'd been at that place so many years without any trouble, they could keep living there. I thought so myself once. Now I know I was wrong. Ginny, I should have warned you."

Paul says, "I thought burning down the barn would help. It wouldn't catch on fire. Guess it was stupid to try."

Herbert chuckles, then his expression turns serious. "Reckon that makes me stupid, too, since I tried three times. Once when I was around eight, another when I was 'bout your age, and the third when Sheldon's daddy died. I know what folks said, but he didn't die from no farm stuff hittin' his head. If you'd checked old newspapers, you woulda known how he died."

"We found out" Ginny says. "We saw him hang himself in the barn."

Herbert jumps and nearly falls off the stump. Paul gets up to help him, but Herbert waves him off.

"We went inside the barn," Ginny says. "It was a vision," Ginny says. "Like a dream, but it seemed real. We saw goats come in and put out Granddaddy's eyes. Then Daddy stepped into the barn and screamed when he saw the body."

"Goats," Herbert mutters. "I'd always wondered how his eyes got poked out."

"Sir?" Ginny says.

"Oh, we were talking about the barn. I tried burning it down with kerosene, gasoline, lighter fluid. Nothing worked. I reckon even if that barn were gone it wouldn't do a lick 'o good. I sneaked inside when I was a boy and found that hole in the ground."

Herbert covers his eyes and falls on the side. Paul and Ginny run up to him and ease him to the ground. Herbert rubs his head, closes his eyes, and he has a pained look on his face. He puts his hands to his face and keeps them there a few seconds until he pulls them back. Susie runs over to join them.

"Damn, man, are you all right?" she asks.

"As okay as I can be with this vivid memory. When I sneaked inside that barn, I wasn't alone in there."

Ginny, Paul, and Susie shiver and draw close to each other.

"Do you feel like you can tell us about it?" Paul asks.

"I have to," Herbert says. "And I'll tell you a great deal more when we get to my house. We'll head there directly."

"Of course you'll go directly. It doesn't make sense to go indirectly," Susie says, and she looks surprised when Paul, Ginny, and Herbert start laughing.

"It's an expression," Ginny says. "*Directly* means *in a*

*little while."*

Susie sighs, "It's like a foreign country down here. I like it anyway, except for evil barns and demons who look like Jesus and shit like that."

That elicits another laugh, but then Mr. Miller speaks in a serious tone.

"I'd better tell you what happened. We need daylight to talk about such things, and time is a'passin.' I was eight-years old when I squeezed through those barn doors at your place, Ginny. Barn wasn't locked tight till after your Grandpa died. I popped inside like a cork, tripped, fell and landed on my face. Part of me I won't mention hit the ground, too, and I writhed in pain for a long time. I moaned but had to stop that, since the sound echoed and scared me.

I don't know how much time passed before I was able to sit up, brush the dust off my clothes and stand. I was finally able to scan the barn with my flashlight. That's when I noticed the hole in the floor. I crept towards it, stopping about five feet from the rim. All at once a grayish-white light lit up the place, lit it up real good. Then a blue flame and smoke came that smelled worse than anything I'd smelled in my short life. Stunk like that gosh-awful sulfur water I had to drink when I visited my Grandma. I held my nose and backed away.

Like an idiot I dropped my flashlight. Luckily there was a crack of sunlight coming in from the front door, and my flashlight lit up part of the floor. I kept backing up until I hit the wall. I sat down and cowered there. I'm tellin' you, a deer in headlights was braver than I was then. A demon came out - red, scaly, with curved horns and thick lips stuck like the smile in one of those masks actors used a long time ago."

Ginny gasps, and Paul's eyes widen. Susie leans so far toward Mr. Miller she looks like a bent tree.

Mr. Miller continues, "Reckon some of you have some familiarity how that thing looked. Not good at all, but I'll get to that directly. The demon hissed at me like a mad cat. *Greetings and salutations, Herbert*, it said. *Welcome to this little portal to my realm. Would you like to join me? For dinner, perhaps?*"

"I couldn't answer, and I couldn't move. About all I could do was squeak 'uuhhs' in in a high-pitched voice, like I'd been sucking on helium. The demon floated toward me, and I pulled my hands over my eyes. It was then that the demon grabbed my arms. I screamed and pulled away, and I'll be doggone if I didn't have bad burns on both those arms. Then the demon got in the mood to talk more. Somehow I could hear it above my screamin', like it was talkin' inside my mind."

"I swear I remember everything it said like it all happened an hour ago. It told me, *You will mind your manners, dear child. Oh, I forgot to introduce myself. How rude. People call me 'The Beast.' Not the kindest term, but I like it. It flies off the tongue quickly as if it is one word: 'The Beast.' You would know me as Satan.*"

"Oh no, we're doomed," Ginny says.

"For sure, if all this is true," Susie says.

"Wait until you hear the rest of the story before you decide the end of the world has come. That demon had a motor mouth once it got started.

"*My real name*, it said, *is 'Light-Bearer,' what you call 'Lucifer' in that language of clerics, Latin. What do you think of my light?"*

"I wasn't too smart, then, but part of me figured that thing would know if I was lying. So I told it, 'Scary... mean... rotten... dead.' Well, if that didn't set the thing off, though it primped its head as if it still had hair. I guess it figured it had to impress me, so it said, *Smart, aren't you? I am Lord of Hell...*

"Then I saw something that I dream about almost every night. Blue flames surrounded that thing's head and started to burn away its flesh. What was left was the most god-awful skull I've ever seen; toothless, no lips of course, but that sarcastic smile still there. It finished the sentence it was working on; *'...and Death.'* Then the flesh flew back to the skull and attached itself, and the head turned back into what it looked like in the first place.

"The thing kept trying to make everything funny, like it took nothing seriously, like it wanted to mock everything; God, the universe, people, itself. I wanted to get out of there, but my legs wouldn't move. Don't know if it was because I was scared or because that demon got ahold of me with some force field. The thing started talking again. I was too young to understand all the words then, but the memory's in my mind like a picture show. It's worse when you understand what that thing means. Would to God I'd stay ignorant.

"*I don't think Mortisifer has quite the ring of Lucifer, do you?* the devil said. I shook my head, but after that skull incident I'd decided to stay quiet. Then the thing says, *Satan got your tongue, I see. Guess what. Today's your lucky day. I'm letting you get out of here alive. You can tell your parents a good lie about the burns. You'll think of something. I'm busy with father Sprigg right now. The Spriggs are too much fun to waste my time with a mere boy. You will tell them nothing, right, boy? Because if you do, I'll come for you in the night, and it won't be a nightmare. You'll be in my world then. Understand?*

"I nodded and figured I needed to say I agreed, so I said, 'Yes, sir.' I know. I called the devil, 'sir.' But I was brought up that way, and I think God may have appreciated that respect I showed for someone who used to be by His side, however messed up he, or *it*, is now. The devil didn't take kindly to it, though. It said, "A polite boy, too. How I hate that." Then it motioned with its hands like it was shooing off a fly. "Shoo, boy, don't bother me," it said. "Go away."

"My legs loosened, and I turned around to find the barn door cracked open. You bet I set a speed record running through that door, hearing that thing's bat-crazy laugh the whole time. I never saw the devil again, though I saw the destruction it wreaked."

Everyone is silent for a moment. Eyes dart around. Paul and Ginny are hugging tightly, and Susie leans against Ginny. They are all trembling.

Finally, Paul speaks. "Is there any way to stop this thing?"

Herbert shakes his head and chuckles. "It's more than a thing. It's the ole' devil, Satan. It said so itself, and I used to think it might be lying, but no more. I'm sure that thing's Satan as sure as I am that this stump I'm sitting on's real. I'll tell you the rest of what I know, but not out here in the open. Maybe together we can figure something out. Let's get inside."

They stand up and begin walking out of the woods. They climb over a fence into a tree-filled front yard.

One tree is filled with peaches. A small, fenced vegetable garden is in the back. Directly ahead is a modest wood frame house.

Paul sighs and says, "I think we're okay for now."

# CHAPTER 14

Sheldon Sprigg, gasping for air, stumbles into the fence dividing his field from the backyard. He falls on his knees, gets up, and climbs over to the other side. He starts to walk and picks up the pace, trying to ignore his throbbing head. Behind him, a demonic figure floats down, morphs into the Jesus-figure, and says, "Sheldon."

Sheldon starts, turns around and bows his head. "I have failed you, Lord," he says. "They were too fast for me, but I have no excuse. I repent in dust and ashes."

"Jesus" replies, "There is still time for you to redeem yourself. Ginny is beyond redemption. There remains no hope of Heaven for her. If she lives she will influence many people to go to hell. You know what you must do."

"I must stop the plague before it spreads," Sheldon says. "I'll use my .22. To make it quick. I don't want her to suffer, at least this side of hell. She is a harlot."

"Yes, she is as bad as the whore of Babylon. She caused you to lust after her."

"Yes, she did," Sheldon says. "If she didn't dress like a slut and wear those thin tops. I never would have torn her blouse. It is all her fault."

"Be sure to bring her to me first," the Beast says. "Inside the barn. That is where you must do it. The barn is a holy place. As steward of the barn, you must be the one to sacrifice Ginny for, the greater good."

Sheldon nods his head. "I will obey you, my Lord and God."

"I promise you," says the Beast. "If you succeed in your appointed task, you may yet avoid meeting your self-murdering father who is now burning in Hell."

"I won't fail you this time, Lord."

✦✦✦

Inside the barn, Satan laughs and talks to himself. "Sheldon, Sheldon, how often do I sift you like wheat, and how often you fall into sin. Ginny's fault for making you lust? You bought into that fast enough. I love getting you to deny that sin is sin. That pisses off the Unmentionable One so much. What shall I do next? Draw you in deeper, through despair. You'll sin again. I'll even play *God's* advocate and tell you that sin is so severe you'll never be forgiven."

Satan finds a rusty file in the barn and sharpens his claws.

✦✦✦

It is late afternoon when Herbert unlocks his door and steps inside his house, followed by Ginny, Paul and Susie. The house is filled with old furniture, bookshelves and scattered papers. Herbert removes some piles of papers off a chair and a couch.

"Sorry about the mess," he says. "I'm writing a history of these parts. Have a seat. I'll bring you some iced tea."

Herbert steps through a door into a kitchen. Paul stands and looks around the room. He picks up some old papers from a desk and thumbs through them.

"God, some of these are almost two-hundred years old."

"Should you be messing around with those papers?" Ginny asks. "If you tear one of them, I'm sure Mr. Miller will be mad."

"He's let me borrow some of his old books before, and some of them were over a hundred years old. We'll be careful, and I don't think he'd mind. There might be some information in those old papers that will help us."

Herbert returns with four glasses of tea on a tray, which he distributes. He sits down, takes his own glass, swallows, and takes a deep breath.

"I should have known I'd get bad news from down the road one day," he says. "I prayed it would never come. If I'd talked to you earlier I would have warned you to watch out for your father acting strange. I messed up on that point, but I won't mess up now. Somehow the devil's been able to get through some kind of portal in that barn, a door between earth and hell that's usually closed, but every so many years it opens. Then the Beast comes through and the owner of that barn, who has always been a Sprigg, goes plumb crazy."

"How often has this happened before," Ginny asks.

"Every time a new generation of Spriggs comes along. That may be coincidence, since they might have children that get old enough for Satan to take over exactly the time that gate opens and the ole' devil slips in."

Paul looks puzzled. "Have you seen any patterns in how this being works?"

Herbert chuckles. "*This being*? Call it what it is -

Satan, the devil, the Beast, Apollyon, Abaddon, whatever. *This being* won't do anymore. We need to realize, and know without a doubt, what we're fighting. If I were Catholic, I'd get a priest, but I'm not. We'll do our best ourselves to send the devil back to hell where he belongs.

"Ginny, you said your father focuses on you being obedient to everything that thing said."

"That's right," Ginny says.

Herbert goes on. "From the time this barn was built, evil and darkness have haunted it. I'm sure it was Satan's doing from the beginning. *It* – from this point forward I will not refer to that thing as a *he* – saw an opportunity to twist a few souls one-on-one and took it.

"The barn was built by Sheldon's great-great granddaddy, Hosea Sprigg, back in 1875. I've read his diary. He said he had a feeling soon as he stepped on the land he'd bought, the barn had to go in that specific place. After the barn was finished, strange things started happening. One day, Hosea touched a sick calf, and it hopped up whole and healthy. Hosea had the gift of healing. He praised God for it and vowed to help people, so he started a ministry. Trouble is, the power was from the wrong person, though at first Hosea used the power for good."

Herbert stands up, walks to a filing cabinet and opens a drawer, thumbing through papers. After a minute passes he pulls a few out.

"Ah, there it is," he says. "An eyewitness account of one of Hosea Sprigg's tent meetings. I'll give you the gist of it. The meeting described is from July 1877. A big tent is spread out in the middle of a field. Outside the tent there was a large sign that said, HOSEA SPRIGG, HEALER. COME ALL, YOUNG AND OLD, TO BE CURED OF YOUR DISEASES. Hosea had his servants - yes, he had grown rich enough to have paid servants - set up wooden benches inside in an orderly way. At the meeting, folks of all ages, rich and poor, black and white - Hosea didn't countenance prejudice – attended. People filled the benches, and some had to stand in the aisles. Some men wore overalls, others business suits. Women wore the best they had, from simple farm dresses to fancy city dresses. Torches and a few large candles lit up the inside of the tent.

"At the front of the tent was a wood stage with a pulpit in the middle. To the cheers of the audience, a young man with a beard wearing a gray suit walked to the stage behind the pulpit. Hosea eyed the cheering crowd, then waved his arms downward to quieten them. Hosea started talking, and everybody got real quiet.

"*It is such a lovely Tennessee night. Welcome. My name is Hosea Sprigg, and I'm doing the Lord's work of healing. Those who have been here before know that I do not demand money for what I do. Those of you who can afford an offering to help me pay expenses can do so should the need strike your heart.*

"Hosea pointed out a person in the audience. *You, sir, where are you from?* he asked. The audience member said, *Cincinnati, Preacher.* Quite a ride by carriage in those days. Hosea pointed to another person. *And you, ma'am, from where did you come?*

"*New York City, Reverend.*

"Now understand, back then people in the South figured Cincinnati was far enough south to be honorary southern. New York City, though it had a lot of southern transplants, was still considered Yankee land. This was twelve years after the 'late unpleasantness' of the War between the States ended. A murmur spread through the crowd, with some voices muttering 'Damn Yankee.'

"Hosea wasn't about to put up with this, so he said, *Brothers and sisters, now is not the time to reopen old wounds. We are all God's children here. Now is the time for healing. You, little girl, in the back. Have your mama and daddy carry you up to the stage.*

"A young black couple carried a girl of about four. She was pale, breathing heavily, and unconscious. There was another murmur in the audience. Reconstruction was a recent memory, and black folks and white folks were mad at each other, blaming one another for the abuses of Reconstruction. It was the whites in power now, and most of them didn't take kindly to black people attending a gathering of whites. Hosea, to his credit, hated those attitudes, and he pushed out his hand to silence the crowd.

"The couple made it to the stage without too much trouble, and Hosea asked, *What, good people, are your names?*

"The man replied, *My name's Moses; this is my wife Mary. Our daughter, her name's Rachel, is dying. Doctor said he can't do anything. She's just five-years old, and she's all we got.*

"*You have good names,* Hosea said. *Give me your daughter.*

"Moses handed Rachel to Hosea, who took her in his arms. Hosea prayed. *Oh God, who canst heal all things by Thy power, place Thy healing hand on this child so that if it be Thy will, she shall be whole again.*

"Immediately after the prayer, Rachel opened her eyes and rubbed them. She was no longer pale. Hosea put her down, and though Mary tried to catch her, Rachel landed on the floor feet first and ran back and forth across the stage. The audience cheered, and some audience members had tears in their eyes.

"That's what happened, and it's obvious that Hosea had a strong notion in his mind to do good. Sadly, the source of his healing power was evil. That's how Satan snagged him; used what Hosea wanted most and twisted it. The devil's getting to your daddy that way, Ginny. Maybe it's scolding Sheldon for something he did that really is wrong, or telling him he can help someone if he accepts the devil's power. Don't know.

"I'll continue the sad story of Hosea. He used his power for good for several years, but the power became a slow-growing cancer inside his soul, eating away his goodness until it corrupted him. He got to the point that he only used it to do evil. A power to heal is a power to affect the body, and if it affects the body the wrong way it can become a power to hurt or kill.

"A local newspaper editor called Hosea a fake, and Hosea wished him dead. At the same time, the editor dropped dead. When Hosea read the obituary giving details of the editor's passing, he put two and two together and figured out he could use his power to kill, and get people out of the way whom he didn't like. After the editor's death people dropped faster than flies in a cloud of Raid. I'll let you read some of the later parts of Hosea's diary."

Herbert turns over a few more pages, then gives the diary to Ginny, who thumbs through it at random.

She stops on a page and starts to read.

"November 5, 1894. Those boys from hell, Tommy and Elton Sanford, sneaked under my fence and messed around in my field today. Eleven and eight and their mama and daddy ain't raised them no better than that. I snared 'em, though, and did my best to scare 'em. Told 'em I'd beat 'em with a stick if I caught them in my field again. I said I was going to slam that stick in their eyes and pin them to the ground. Told 'em I preferred trespassers dead, 'specially little boys. If they don't get the message from that I will beat them with a stick."

"Sounds like a bitter old man," Ginny says. "Like Mr. Morton was before he died. He'd get mad if I kicked a ball over his fence and had to climb the fence to get it. He said I was trespassing and would call the sheriff. He told me he'd sic his goats on me, and that they had sharp horns that would gut me. He did phone the sheriff, but that time Daddy's knowing the deputies helped. Then Daddy went to Mr. Morton's house and 'persuaded' him to leave me alone if I had a good reason to be on his land. I have a feeling his 'persuasion' included threats."

"At least Ben Morton had an excuse for being bitter," Herbert said. "Tortured by the Viet Cong when he was in that awful Vietnam War. Never got over that.

"But back in the old days, Hosea had changed into a man meaner than snot. Had to have had it in him, even when he was doing good. Satan only expands what's already in a person, making the good part smaller and the evil part bigger. Read the next entry in the diary."

Ginny begins reading. "November 6, 1894: This

morning I was walking through my field and found my bull dead by the fence line. He'd been shot dead. Children's footprints were in the mud. I reckon those Sanford boys went squirrel hunting and decided to get me back for tellin' 'em off yesterday. Well, they got into my field for the last time. Killin' my cattle, my property. I figured it was a good time to visit my barn, so I went there immediately to meet the Preacher. The old man wore his usual black suit and tie and held his Bible in his left hand. Always found that odd, but he helps me out a lot, so I overlook it. I shook his hand and told him those Sanford boys were giving me trouble, sneaking into my field and killing my bull. Told him I'd have to buy a new bull to be a sire. I asked the Preacher the best way to visit God's justice on those boys. He said, in his usual high-falutin' tone, 'Fellow servant of the true God of this World, God's wrath is upon those boys. God is willing to do whatever you request.' I told the Preacher, 'I request an unfortunate accident.' I'm grateful that he told me, 'God shall grant your request tonight.'"

Ginny drops the diary on the table as if it's a book of curses.

Herbert takes a deep breath and says, "That evening at twilight, a horse pulling a small buggy strode around a sharp curve. 'Course it was a dirt road back then, and horses and buggies stirred up dust that made it hard to see. Some people drove reckless back then, too, like they do today in automobiles. Tommy and Elton Sanford sat in the back of that little buggy.

"Meanwhile, Mitch Pearcy had taken his horse and buggy to Randallsville to buy some feed. On his way back something spooked his horses, though later he said he saw nothing in the area that would cause them to take off the way they did. They took the curve too fast, and he was able to keep the buggy on the road, but was not able to avoid a head-on route toward the Sanford buggy. The Sanford's horses reared to get out of the way, and the Sanford buggy tumbled down an embankment.

"The irony, the irony. Hosea preached their funerals. I once knew an older lady who was in the crowd as a young girl, and she said she saw an old man wearing a black suit standing in the crowd with 'the most awful smile on his face I've ever seen.' She went back to her family's carriage, and saw Hosea standing alone at the graves. Her mama said he was crying, but she thought he was laughing. The little girl cried out and ran inside the carriage when she saw 'the devil himself, scaly, red, toothless, and smiling.'"

There is a long moment of silence. Clocks tick loudly, and everyone jumps when a "coo-coo" sounds five times. Herbert breaks the silence.

"There was no justice for those young boys. Hosea died a peaceful death in his sleep in 1922. The doctor said it was a stroke and that he never felt a thing."

Susie stands up and starts to pace. "So that evil bastard demon makes good people bad."

"Or a bad person worse," says Paul. "Like the One Ring in the *Lord of the Rings*. Except this time it's for real."

"That's right," Herbert says. "I imagine the magic ring in the story you're talking about drew a person to it?"

"Yes," said Paul. "It seemed to be good at first but was utterly evil."

"Even Satan himself appeareth as an angel of light.

But how the Devil tempts a person depends on the person's character. I suppose when it appears directly to a person, as it does in the barn, Satan gives folks too much power for them to handle. Even Hosea, who started out almost a saint, turned to darkness. At the end of his life, his heart was as rotten as a maggot-filled corpse.

"Hosea had three children. Ginny, the one who survived past childhood, was your Great-Granddaddy, Marshall Sprigg. I have a photo of him."

Herbert gets up and opens a drawer on an antique desk. He looks through some envelopes, finds the one he wants, and thumbs through the contents. He takes out a photo and passes it to Ginny before returning to his seat. Ginny looks at it. The photograph is of a man wearing a black suit, a black tie and a black fedora, posing by a tree. His face is thin, skull-like, his eyes dark like empty sockets. His mouth is slightly open in a frown. Ginny drops the photo and covers her eyes. Paul puts his hand on her shoulder. Susie picks the photo up but immediately turns it face-down on her lap.

"Mother of God, what a creepo," Susie says. "That man looks like he'd been dead thirty years when that pic was taken. What did he do for a living, act in a zombie show? Are you sure this isn't one of those pics people used to take of people after they died? They'd pose them in chairs, stand them up on hidden hooks, all to give the family a first pic of their dead relative, you know, the one they really didn't like that much and never took to a photographer."

"You shouldn't be so cynical," Paul says. "Most of those photos were of recently deceased children."

"I've seen a fake Jesus, my best friend's father turning into a devil-possessed loon, heard stories that make the best of people seem evil, and now I've just seen Skeletor."

"So have we all," says Paul.

"This is not a photograph of a dead man," Herbert says. "He was living and active when this photo was taken."

Ginny sits in the chair, her head back, her eyes closed. Susie notices her and says, "Hey, Ginny, you okay?"

Ginny opens her eyes, stares at the face-down photo, and sighs. "That freaked me out - that I descended from that... soulless thing."

"Can't pick your relatives," Susie says. The others laugh, and Ginny is glad to have Susie here to keep the horror from overwhelming her and the others.

"Good for you," Herbert says. "We needed that, but soon we won't have time to laugh if this mess goes the course it usually does. Marshall had a soul once, but turned greedy. Ole' Satan took that flaw and made it into a hunger so that the more money he made, the thinner and hungrier he became. He didn't care how he got his money. He started a garment factory where he hired children as young as six. He made them eat their lunch while they worked. His legacy was half-starved workers dying from exhaustion and being fired for "inability to work." He forced his employees to shop for shoddy items at inflated prices at the company store. He was a murderer like his father, too."

"Murder?" Ginny says. "Do you mean the workers he killed through neglect?"

"Not at all," Herbert said. "He killed one individual with malice aforethought."

"How do you know that's true," Paul asks.

"Marshall told me himself," Herbert says "on his deathbed. He wasn't trying to clear his conscience. He was bragging. He murdered his wife and got away with it. I suppose it fits, Satan influencing a man to kill. I think Jesus said somewhere that Satan was 'a murderer from the beginning,' a passage that always scared the hell out of me since it reads like Jesus spoke from memory, from personally knowing Satan. The history of the barn is a history of murder, of blood spilled that can never quench the devil's thirst. Like Sheldon, Satan's never satisfied. It wouldn't have mattered, Ginny, if you hadn't gone to that bar and had stayed home from the dance. Sheldon would have found some other minor point to nail you, and the devil would have built that up in Sheldon's mind until it ate out what was left of his common sense.

"Back to the story. The most horrific part of the history is something Jeb Morton told me not long before he died. He was the father of the Mr. Morton who served in 'Nam and had a pen full of goats. That demon would possess those goats from time to time and they'd run plumb crazy. Sometimes they'd get loose and go after somebody, who'd call the sheriff."

Ginny jumps in. "When Susie and I were in the barn, we saw goats gouge out my granddaddy's eyes."

Herbert nods and continues, "Jeb stopped to visit Marshall about selling some of his farmland. He passed by the barn and noticed the door was open. He looked inside and saw Marshall kiss... let me tell you the whole story before I get to that part.

"The very first part of the story I culled from Marshall's notebook. He liked to brag on his misdeeds and wanted people to find out about those deeds after he died. I don't remember how I got ahold of that notebook, but part of me regrets that I did. Gathered from the notebook and what Marshall told me is this: the time was October 1919. Elizabeth, Marshall's wife, sleeps in their bedroom. Moonlight streams through a bedroom window and lands on Liz. A shadow hovers behind her. The shadow reveals himself as a human body with a hideous skull-like face; Marshall. In his hands is a rope in shape of a noose tied with a hangman's knot. He slips the rope around her head, gently lifting her head so as not to awaken her. He pulls the rope tight.

"Elizabeth sits up, struggles, as Marshall holds the rest of the rope at a distance. The more Elizabeth moves, the tighter the noose. She gags and makes gurgle-like sounds. Her body twitches convulsively for some time, but then jerks one last time and stays still. A high-pitched sound, as of air moving through a tiny space, escapes her lips. It takes another ten minutes for her heart to beat its last, and the whole time Marshall had his ear to her chest, like he enjoys listening to her die. Marshall pulls Elizabeth's body out of the bedroom, down the stairs, out the back door, across the grass, into the barn. He walks over to some farm tools stacked against the back wall and searches them. He then looks up - there is an ax hanging on a nail. He takes the ax, walks over to the body, and chops off the head. Blood trickles from the body, adding to the vast amounts on the floor. Marshall takes the head and throws it down the hole.

Then he drags the body by the feet and rolls it into the hole. The blood disappears from the place he'd dragged the body as if it were never there.

"A beautiful young woman with black hair approaches Marshall. She takes Marshall's hands and holds them. She tells him, *You have done well, my love.* Marshall and the woman kiss passionately. He lowers her to the barn floor. His eyes are closed. The woman turns into Satan and continues the kiss. Marshall says, *My darling, you have such full lips!* Satan answers, using the woman's voice. *I can do more than kiss with them. Keep your eyes shut.* I won't go any further than tellin' you that, but after they were done, Satan tells Marshall to open his eyes. Satan is there in his demonic form. It laughs, still using the woman's voice. Marshall screams until he passes out."

Herbert looks down to find Ginny, Susie and Paul huddled together shivering on the floor. Beads of sweat cover Ginny's brow.

Even Paul has paled, but he manages to say, "Mr. Miller, I'm glad you're not a boy scout troop leader. You would scare the poor guys to death with your stories. And to think that this one is true. O man, this sucks."

"It's gross," Susie says. "OMG! You mean this guy had Satan do... oh, shit. No wonder his soul left his body before he died. I feel like puking thinking about it."

"You see the world I've lived in for 75 years," Herbert says. "It's a wonder I'm still *well-preserved*, as the ladies at the Senior Center like to say."

"Oh, they just want to get... oops. Sorry," Susie says, but Herbert laughs.

"Don't worry. I'll take it as blessed comic relief," Herbert says. "Lordy Mercy, that fed my ego."

Ginny gasps, trying to push out the mental image from the story that makes her skin crawl like a colony of snakes. "Those two didn't have children, I hope," she says.

"No, thank God," Herbert says, "and I'm pretty sure of that. No stories about Satan's children sucking blood from babies around here. Satan has enough bloodsuckers in Washington, DC."

"Could this evil be inherited?" Susie asks. "Ginny, you haven't thought that you?" She stops talking, then covers her mouth with one hand.

"Of course not!" Ginny says, with a sting in her voice. "You heard Mr. Miller. Satan and his demons only bring out the evil that is in a person if he gets too close. I suppose it means you have to invite the devil to live inside you."

"That's the traditional doctrine of possession," Paul says. "Without an invitation, demons cannot directly enter someone."

"I agree," Herbert says. "Those who are evil yield first, but good people, thinking they will do greater good, fall for the trap Satan sets as well. We know that this demon can change shape into authority figures that a person fears and respects. If one of these illusions convinces somebody they're the real deal, then..."

"...we get Daddy," Ginny finishes.

"And the whole time your daddy's soul continues to rot," Paul says. "He will end up human remains and not a real person, even though his body may still be alive. Satan has many names for a good reason. He's only fragments, not a complete person. I guess that's why Mr. Miller calls him *it*. I'd hate to see your daddy turn out like that, Ginny, but if he comes after you and I have to kill him, I will."

Susie laughs. "Why do you have to be so pompous, Paul? Okay, so Satan's a bad dude, he has some kind of personality disorder, he tells Sheldon to do bad things, and you'll shoot Sheldon if he comes after Ginny. I said what you said, but better."

Ginny can't help but laugh. *Vintage Susie.*

Herbert smiles and says, "Paul and Ginny, you have wisdom beyond your years," Herbert says. "Ginny, don't you let this young man go."

Ginny turns to Paul and kisses him on the cheek.

"I don't plan on it," she says. Paul blushes deep red, and he and Ginny kiss long and hard on the lips. Herbert smiles and turns away. Susie rolls her eyes and stares at the ceiling.

The room begins to grow dark. Thunder booms in the distance. Herbert walks to the window and gazes outside.

"Storm's a'coming," he says. "In the past, storms have been bad omens when the devil is active here." Herbert walks back and forth, rubbing his head. "We're dealing with nonhuman evil," he says, "the kind that seizes a man's soul in the night and kills his goodness, leaving behind a demonic shell. Ginny, your grandpa, Jacob Sprigg. Do you know why he killed himself?"

Ginny shakes her head. "I don't know, but I'm sure the Beast drove him to do it."

Herbert leans over, speaks in a low voice, as

shadows lengthen in the room, and a flash of lightning and a clash of thunder send Ginny into Paul's arms. Susie turns on the lamp. There is another flash of lightning and a louder thunderclap, and the lamp goes out. A faint, shadowy light remains in the room, and Susie moves down to the floor and sits close to Ginny and Paul. Ginny reaches down and squeezes her shoulder.

Herbert opens a cabinet and pulls out an old-fashioned oil lamp, which he lights and sets on a table. He takes a chair and pulls it beside the others and sits down.

"Don't worry, young'uns," he says. "We'll make it out of this mess if we have to dig a hole to China with our fingernails."

"Eww!" Susie says.

They all laugh. Herbert looks to Susie and says, "You may be a little bad, you may have a smart mouth, but I'm glad God made you."

This time Susie blushes, and Ginny stifles the urge to say something smart herself. A horror of a great darkness descends into her heart when the truth strikes her that they may not get out of this nightmare alive. They may all be killed, or all live, or some may live to mourn the dead. She imagines Paul in a casket, then Susie, then Mr. Miller, then herself, the lips sewn shut, the skin's death-pale tone hidden by the funeral parlor's soft light near the casket. The thought of loss pulls her away to hide in herself, and just as she starts to sag into sleep, Mr. Miller continues his story.

"About Jacob Sprigg," Herbert says. "He was the spitting image of his pa, in more ways than one."

Herbert takes a photo out of a drawer and shows it

to Ginny. Susie cranes her neck down, and Paul leans over for a look.

The photo shows a man more skeletal than his father. Black eyes with unnaturally wide pupils stare straight ahead. Above his head a flock of starlings passes by. The trees that border the field in which his photo was taken are bare, with claw-branches clutching the sky. The effect is three-dimensional.

Ginny feels as if the photo is going to draw her inside, and she averts her eyes. Herbert glances over at Ginny and turns the photo over.

"I always thought about getting rid of this picture even though Jacob was family," he says. Ginny looks at Herbert, her eyebrows furrowed and her eyes open wide. "I should have told you before, Ginny; we are distant cousins, second cousins twice removed, as they say these days, what we used to call fourth cousins. I'll tell you more when this mess is over. You see, I'm caught up in it more than you might think.

"I'm ashamed to tell you I wanted to trash this photograph, since I knew Jacob all too well. When I was twelve, we were walking back with our rods and reels from Simmons Creek where we'd gone fishing. I also carried a small tackle box and Jacob carried a bucket with the fish we caught; five or six rockfish, if I remember rightly. All of a sudden Jacob stopped in his tracks. He asks me, *Want to see something really gross?*

"I didn't share his liking for disgusting things, but he was a cousin, albeit distant, and I had to take care. *I don't know*, I said.

"Jacob took my 'I don't know' as a 'yes' and said *Watch this!* He took a switchblade knife out of his pocket. Don't know how he gotta hold of something like that. From one of his mean friends at school, I reckon. He set the fish bucket down and dipped his hand inside, bringing out a fish that wriggled on the ground. He took that knife and sliced it open, and there it all was - the fish's still-beating heart and innards all a pulsing. The fish kept wriggling as Jacob held it down. I hated Jacob being so cruel to a fish I figured must be feeling everything he's doing. *Stop it! That's mean! You can't hurt that poor fish like that.*

"*Are you a wimp? A chicken?* Jacob asked. *What's the difference between cutting up a fish when it's alive and a hook in its mouth when it's alive? It's just a fish. Ain't worth anything more than for eatin'.*

"*But you take out the hook soon as you can,* I said. *And when you clean a fish, you cut off its head first so it won't suffer.*

"Jacob ignored me and kept cutting up the fish. The heart still beat, but it got slower, and the fish didn't move around as much. I prayed it had stopped feeling pain. Still, I was madder than an old wet hen, and I wanted Jacob to get in trouble. The only stupid thing I did was tell Jacob what I planned. I said, *I'm going to tell your Ma and Pa on you.*

"That sure as heck did it. Jacob took me by the collar, tore open my shirt, grabbed the knife he used to cut the fish, and sliced me from sternum to belly button. I collapsed, crying and scared I'd die right then and there in the middle of nowhere. Jacob ran away, the wicked little coward, singing to the tune of *na na na na boo boo* this charming little song:

*I killed a chicken,*
*I killed a chicken.*
*Tonight I'll have chicken dinner,*

*Tonight I'll have chicken dinner.*

"If I had died and the evil brat came back, it's no telling what he would have done to me. Jacob might have eaten Herbert stew for supper."

"Shit! How did you live?" Susie asks.

"Lucky for me he didn't cut that deep. While Jacob was ranting I tied what was left of my shirt over the worst part of the wound and staggered into the woods. I fell, rolled down a hill, and Jacob never found me. I crawled and scooted my way back to my folk's house. Put me in the hospital two weeks, that did. Jacob was sent to reform school in Nashville for two years. Like most reform schools, this one made him meaner than ever. When he got out, all hell broke loose."

"Daddy said Granddaddy was wild when he was young," Ginny says.

*"Wild,"* he said? "How about child molester? Rapist. Thief. Murderer. The man had lots of money, for sure, ill-gotten, from thievin' and moonshinin.' He hired trained killers to murder his rivals. Bribed the judges and juries, he did, and didn't spend a lick of time in prison. Strange thing is, he had a twisted sense of justice. Said a fellow he knew had been a judge in New Orleans and was givin' him advice. I figure that was the disguise the devil used with him.

"Jacob finally settled down with your grandma. I have to give him credit only this far; he felt guilty and that guilt got worse and worse over time. Good to know your Granddaddy wasn't one of those psychopaths. He knew he'd never paid for his crimes. The devil works that way sometimes; kills the conscience for a time and allows it to revive only to cause despair and pain. Remember the story of Judas, the apostle who betrayed Christ. He felt guilty, even returned the blood money he was paid. Instead of changing his life for the better, he despaired and hung himself. After he hung for awhile the rope broke, and the Book of Acts says he fell down headfirst and all his guts spilled out.

"Sounds a lot like Jacob Sprigg. One evening, 'bout thirty years ago, he came by my house. I had no idea who was dropping by when I heard a knock at the door at seven. Usually folks don't visit that late without calling first. Well, I opened the door and there was Jacob Sprigg, looking like he'd already been in hell for a few years. Though he'd never exactly said he was sorry for cutting me, we had an unspoken agreement to be civil toward each other. So I said, *Well I'll be doggone. Jacob. We're cousins and neighbors, but I haven't seen you in ages. You look rough today.*

Dad burn it if Jacob didn't start crying. That sure shocked me. I never saw him cry before, not at funerals, nowhere. He wiped his eyes with a dirty handkerchief. I felt sorry for him and gave him another one. *Just throw that old one in the trash*, I said. He had the hardest time saying anything, his voice broke so much, but here's what I understood.

"*I'm unforgivable*, he said. *A human monster. I'm sorry for everything. God's sorry He let me be born. Why'd I cut you, Herb? That was so mean. And the worse things I done after, horrible murders, taking advantage of innocent children, O God! Lord, forgive me. I pray for forgiveness every day, but I know He can't forgive me for what I've done. I'm gonna miss that sweet bye and bye and burn in those hot flames. I dream about 'em all the time. Boils bubbling up, screaming, demons all around smiling at me, sticking me with those pitchforks. See, devil's already got me, and he won't let me go. No matter what happens, I'm damned, a lost soul.*

"As bad as he'd been in his life, I didn't want him to end up in that hot hell. I showed him kindness, put my hand on his shoulder and led him to the couch. I poured him some iced tea and left the pitcher out so he could have his fill. He took a few sips, then hung his head. Lord knows I tried to reason with him. I told him, *You know your Bible enough to know God can forgive you for anything. You look sorry for what you did, but have you fully repented?*

"Jacob shook his head back and forth to communicate 'no,' and his head would jerk from time to time like he had the tics.

"*I gotta die now*, he said. *Ain't no hope in this life. My wife would be better off without me. Sheldon, m'dear son, don't need no bad example like me for a daddy.*

"I could see why he could feel that way, but it's silly to throw your life away and not make the best of what's left, no matter how bad off you are. This life's short 'nough as it is. So I told him, *Now you're talking nonsense. There ain't any need to kill yourself. Repent, apologize to your family, and to your victims' families like you did to me. Go to the police and take the consequences. I doubt the inmates would pick on an old man like you. There's a chapel in the penitentiary, and you can pray there. It'll be shameful; I'd be a durned fool to deny that. I'm telling you the truth, though, that if you confess everything, you'll feel better. Your victims' families will say some nasty things, and neither you nor I should blame them. Some of them are better Christians than I would be, and some of that group will forgive you. You need to do what it takes for God to forgive you. You can set a good example in the penitentiary. I don't doubt one bit that God will forgive everything you've done and that you'll find rest in that sweet bye and bye.*

"I thought I'd done a good job trying to knock some sense into Jacob's head. But I was asking him to do hard things, and he couldn't live with the shame. He told me, *Sheldon don't need to see his daddy arrested, put on trial for murder, found guilty, and put in jail or killed in the 'lectric chair. He don't need to know that Old Sparky was my last companion. I gotta see Jesus now so I can be judged and go to hell.*

"*I can't let you do this*, I said, but Jacob stood up and shuffled his way to the door. *Gotta go, Herb*, he said. *You take care, now.*

"Then I did the damnedest fool thing I ever did in my life. I told him, *Take care of yourself, Jacob. Don't hurt yourself.* I should've taken him to a hospital; dragged him by the feet if I had to. I know they wouldn't have done much, kept him on suicide watch for a day, but it was better than what I did. The last thing Jacob said to me was, *Already hurt m'self more than I can take.* He walked away into the dying of the light at the end of the day. God, why didn't you put any more sense in my head?

"But I did one thing. I picked up the phone and called the sheriff. Heck of a lot of good that did. Nobody paid attention in those days. Sheriff's office wouldn't send a deputy. I tried to keep an eye on ole' Jacob, asked some neighbors to do the same. Three days later he was dead, and you know how. I messed up there."

"You did the best you could at the time," Ginny says. "I think he was going to kill himself no matter what anybody did. All a hospital might have done is put it off a few days."

"One of my uncles was in the hospital on suicide watch," Susie says. "He had post-traumatic stress disorder from his time in Iraq. I think he had to kill a six-year old girl holding a grenade. She was about to pull the pin and kill herself and my uncle and the men with him. He saved their lives, but he shot the girl in the head, and some of her brains flew into his face. He couldn't live with a world in which he had no choice but to shoot a child. The VA released him after three days. His wife and their relatives and friends kept an eye on him, but he was able to sneak out of the house and walk into an outbuilding. I don't know what it takes in a man for him to put a rope around his neck, jump down, and let it close off his air. Pathologist said he lived about fifteen minutes after he started hanging. Those knots have to be perfect to break the neck, and my uncle, and I hate to put it this way, was an amateur."

"Oh, God." Susie sobs once, then regains control and looks at Herbert. "Mr. Miller, you did fine by your cousin. He decided to do what he did, and he's responsible. Maybe God will help him change after death. I don't know much about religious things other than what my priest says, but I believe God is merciful. He's not your father's God, Ginny."

"Thank God for that," Ginny says and the others laugh.

"I've been thinking about the goats who attacked

Mr. Sprigg's body," Paul says. I bet all of you know that the goat is one traditional symbol of Satan."

"I suppose the devil did get him in the end in that respect," Ginny says.

"Yep," Herbert says. "Sad in a way despite all the awful things Jacob did."

"I can't deal with much more *awful* today," Susie says.

"No choice," Ginny says. "We'll get it done, partner. We'll help the devil get back to where he belongs." She and Susie make fists and bang them together.

Ginny turns to Herbert. "Do you think Daddy's real character was drawn out by the demon?"

"Sheldon tried to be too good," Herbert says. "The Beast took advantage of that. You know that Bible verse, Ecclesiastes I think, that says, "Be not righteous overmuch." Sheldon overdid the overmuch."

"It corrupted him," Paul says, "made him self-righteous, legalistic, a Pharisee in the worst sense of the word. He reasoned well from his starting points; took them to their logical conclusion. He found his reason only to lose his human feelings."

"So he's a fucking possessed robot," Susie says, and after blushing deeply, she continues, "er, excuse me, Mr. Miller."

Herbert laughs. "I heard worse than that in my life. But you're right, that's exactly what Sheldon is. Don't think of him as your daddy any more, Ginny. What remained of most of the good in him died when that fake Jesus showed up, but he really died as a child when he saw that black and blue face and goat-eaten eyes on his daddy's body when it hung in that barn. He thought his daddy died because of disobedience to

God. And by God, Sheldon was going to be different. He would obey God with dotted i's and crossed t's."

Ginny speaks slowly. "So God became..."

"...the devil," Herbert says. "At least in Sheldon's eyes, though he doesn't see it that way. Sheldon is a Satanist without knowing it, worshipping a demonic evil who surveys the world with an all-seeing eye, waiting to catch someone doing wrong so He can torture that person in hell. He'll tell the person to do worse things or make him feel so guilty for his crimes it drives him to despair and suicide."

Susie huffs and says, "That really sucks rancid c..."

"Susie!" Ginny interrupts.

Herbert smiles and says, "That's also about the right way to put it."

# CHAPTER 15

There is a flash of lightning and a crash of thunder. For a split second, the room shines bright as day. A shadowy figure appears by the windowsill. The outline of a pitchfork is clearly seen in the shadow's hand. Ginny screams. There are loud knocks on the door, and Sheldon's voice booms above the thunderclaps.

"Let me in, old man. Stop interfering with my daughter's discipline or I'll send you straight to hell."

"Get back, young'uns," Herbert says. "I'll take care of this."

He moves to a dusty corner of the room and grabs his .12-gauge shotgun, checks it to make sure it is loaded, and moves between the window and the rest of the group. Ginny, Paul and Susie stand back but remain in the room. The sound of glass breaking startles everyone but Herbert, and the teens jump back, taking cover behind chairs and the couch. The blinds fall, strewn aside by the rusty prongs of a pitchfork.

Sheldon Sprigg steps into the room, turns around, and slams the wooden end of the pitchfork on the floor. His mouth is twisted into a hideous scowl, and he reaches Herbert, towering over him like a clawed Nosferatu. He raises the pitchfork, aims it at Herbert, and rams it toward Herbert's stomach. Herbert falls to the side, avoiding the blow, and fires his shotgun. A few pellets strike Sheldon on the arm. Sheldon does not react, but from behind him the Jesus-figure darts and stands beside him. The demon's mouth widens, and a sword hilt emerges. The faux Jesus pulls the sword from his mouth and raises it in the air. A lightning flash kindles the sword into a blinding flame of light.

"Sheldon, you fool!" Herbert shouts, his words like rapids flowing fast over cragged rocks. "Can't you see that thing ain't Jesus! He looks like that painting of Jesus that's in so many King James Bibles. It's Satan! The devil! The Beast! He's after your soul and drives you to murder. Open your eyes to the truth. This is the creature who murdered your daddy. Drove him to hang himself." Herbert points directly at the false Jesus. "This is the one to fight, not us."

The Beast, retaining its Jesus shape, hisses like a snake and rises into the air, gliding around Sheldon and Herbert and reaching Ginny. He seizes her by the throat with his right hand and carries her toward Sheldon. She gags and grabs the devil's hands, but they stay taut, and she cries out, pulls her hands away, and finds blisters from the heat of the devil's claws.

The devil pushes his face toward Ginny, and she gags on his hot sulfur breath. The devil says, "Now you will face the price of your disobedience, child. You will go with your father into the barn, and he will administer the sentence. Then you shall stay with me forever, where we'll live happily ever after."

The beast tousles Ginny's hair and grins. The demon-mouth appears with its smile of pure sarcasm and spite. Ginny screams and struggles. Satan holds Ginny high in the air and begins to float toward the broken window. Blinds lift on their own, and Ginny and the beast pas over most of the broken glass until the beast shifts, pulling Ginny toward a shard of glass sticking out like a canine tooth. She lifts her legs, and the glass tooth barely misses cutting her feet. Herbert aims his gun, but the devil turns Ginny around to face Herbert, and he lowers his gun.

"You son of a whore," Herbert says.

Satan stands outside, his Jesus-face grinning at Herbert. Sheldon jumps out the window, partially blocking a clear view of the Beast. Feet disappear into the sky, and Herbert leaps out the window, with Paul and Susie following close behind. Sheldon laughs maniacally. Blood drips from his pellet wounds like red raindrops.

Herbert raises his gun and asks, "Where has it taken her?"

"It?" Sheldon asks. "It? You call my Lord by that word, you wicked old coot? Don't worry. You'll see Ginny again. When you join her in hell!"

Herbert points the gun at Sheldon's feet and pulls the trigger. There is a *click*, but the gun fails to fire. Herbert slams the gun into the ground and says, "Doggone it, I knew I needed more shells in that gun."

Sheldon runs away, heading towards the barn. The rest of the group stands in the dimming light of early evening. Herbert peers into the distance. Susie shakes so hard she slips to the ground and grabs her head.

"Oh God, Ginny, God, God, God..."

Paul tries to run, but Herbert takes him by the collar and pulls him back.

"Why'd you do that?" Paul says, balling his hands into fists.

Herbert shakes Paul. "If you go after them by yourself it won't help Ginny, and you'll end up being six feet under. I'll go to the barn. This is way too dangerous for you two."

"No!" Paul says. "I have to go with you."

"Me, too!" Susie says.

Herbert turns to Paul and raises his voice. "Stay with Susie, boy. Go to the bathroom, lock the door, and don't come out until I come back, hear? If you two go up there by yourselves, you'll put Ginny in more danger than she's in already. You may get all of us killed. Trust me on this, okay?"

Paul huffs and shakes his head.

"Didn't you hear me? Do as I say! Time's a'wastin.'"

"But that monster will kill Ginny. I love her. I have to save her."

Herbert puts his hands on Paul's shoulders and squeezes them. "I know, but you need to stop pretending you're a knight in shining armor. I've got a dead man on my conscience already and ain't having the deaths of two children on my conscience. Get inside the house. Please."

"He's right, Paul," Suzie says. "Mr. Miller has more experience dealing with that monster. We have to trust him."

"I hate this," Paul says, but he bows his head and walks with Susie toward the door.

The sky is clearing, and the slight light of the dying

evening illuminates Herbert's path to a building in the back, which he unlocks with a key on his chain. He looks around in some drawers until he pulls out a box of shotgun shells. He loads the chamber to the max and drops the remaining shells into a pocket in his overalls.

"May not work on you, Satan," he mutters to himself, "but they sure as hell will work on Sheldon."

# CHAPTER 16

The beast floats in front of the barn, holding a struggling Ginny in his arms. The lock clicks, and the chains fall off on their own. The door creaks open, and Satan, still shape-shifted to look like Jesus, floats in. It still holds Ginny by the throat. It whispers something vile in her ear. She does not hear it as words, but as a whispered mixture of a snake hiss and a buzzard cry. She screams louder when she sees the steam rising from a new burn and feels the ache of new pain.

She pulls her emotions back as much as she can and tries to think. *I'd better stop fighting him unless I can find some way to escape. Satan's hands only burn when I make an aggressive move. They don't burn when it squeezes my neck. Small comfort. Death by fire or death by suffocation – take my pick, right?*

Ginny gags, but realizes that Satan will probably let Sheldon finish her off. Maybe her friends will come to help, but she fears putting them at risk. Mr. Miller will surely come if Sheldon hasn't already killed him. She struggles to breathe, wheezes enough air to remain conscious, and says a silent prayer for herself and her friends.

"Time to feed," says the Beast. Satan laughs and begins to speak in a sing-song voice. "Oh, Sheldon, time to do your thing."

Sheldon runs inside the barn, stops, holding his hands to his stomach and gasping for air. The barn doors slowly close. There is the sound of metal clanging and a lock clicking.

✝ ✝ ✝

Elma, wearing a modest dress, lies on the couch in her living room. She mulls over the madness of the past few days and makes a decision. She married Sheldon twenty years ago after knowing him since primary school. He was a good husband and kept his worst traits at bay until six months ago. He had always been overly strict, and Elma sensed a lack of love in some of his condemnation of other people's sins. Still, he once had a merciful streak. When Ginny kissed a boy she had a crush on in seventh grade, Sheldon yelled at Ginny, who ran up to her room and cried. Later, he walked upstairs and apologized. He took the time to explain why he didn't approve of what she did. No more does he show mercy.

Elma worries that Sheldon has gone mad. Sometimes she wonders whether he is demon-possessed. It seems like some foreign presence has invaded his mind. She loves him, but she does not love the thing he is becoming, and she can no longer put Ginny at risk. Elma thinks she can handle Sheldon herself if he becomes violent, but Ginny will be in danger. A legal separation with a temporary restraining order seems the best option to seek. She does not want a divorce. She doesn't believe in divorce. But if Sheldon hurts Ginny again, Elma feels she will have no choice.

A scream screeches through her ears, and she jumps to attention, her heart pounding. She clutches her chest and sits up on the couch, listening.

"Ginny?" she says. There is another scream. She knows the voice. Ginny's voice.

"O dear God," she says, and she hurries to a drawer and grabs a set of keys, placing them in the pocket of her dress. Then she snags a shotgun from a rack on the wall, checks the shells inside, opens the door, and runs outside. She rushes toward the barn and stops beside it. She surveys it. Nothing seems out of the ordinary. She listens for any trace of a sound. There is none. A large group of vultures startles her as they fly toward the barn, screeching a death's head hymn. They get louder, and Elma puts her hands over her ears, letting the shotgun slide to the ground. When the vultures land on the barn roof, she knows they smell death's approach inside. Picking up the shotgun, she runs toward the barn door.

When Elma reaches the door, she clutches the shotgun against her body with one arm and takes the keys out of her pocket with the other. Ginny's screams grow louder, and Elma struggles to find the right key. She tries three of them, but none work. Then a large, weathered hand touches her shoulder and she spins around, leveling the shotgun at Herbert Miller's face. He raises his hands and backs away. Elma lowers the gun and lets out her held breath, feeling her heart skip a beat.

"You're lucky I didn't send you to heaven with this

shotgun," she says. "You startled me half to death. But thank God you're here. I heard Ginny scream and she was scared for her life."

"I need to get inside the barn," Herbert says. "What's behind all of this is pure evil. Ginny is inside that barn, and Sheldon, along with something far more dangerous, is holding her hostage. Don't bother calling the police. Trust me – they wouldn't believe us. I'm sure that devil is smart enough to split as long as they are here, and as soon as they left, that bastard would be back."

Elma fumbles with her keys again. "We've gotta get in there now! I can't find the right key. Please help me." She throws the keys on the ground and says, "It's too dark," and she starts to cry.

Herbert puts a hand on her shoulder and says, "I have a light." He reaches into his pocket, pulls out his keys, and turns on the penlight attached to the keyring.

Elma picks up the keys, looks through them again and says, "There it is." She inserts the key into the lock, and it clicks open.

Together they pull away the chain and lift the handle. The doors crack. Herbert motions Elma behind him and takes the lead to look inside, making sure his shotgun leads the way. He flicks a light switch, and starts when the lights come on. There is no sign of the Jesus-figure, Sheldon or Ginny. Elma follows him as he steps inside. Herbert looks up at the light near the ceiling.

"Bulb looks fresh, like it's been changed recently," he says. He glances at Elma, notices her gun, and says

"That shotgun you're holding. What's the gauge?"

"20," she says.

"I've got a 12-gauge. It's got a wider range than yours."

They survey the barn. There is no sign of anyone else. Muffled screams seem to come from a great distance, but they get louder and echo eerily through the barn. Herbert cocks his ear and says, "They're coming from that hole."

Elma lunges toward the hole, but Herbert catches her by the arm and pulls her back.

"You have to keep your head on straight," Herbert says. "You go full speed toward that hole you might fall in."

Out of the hole floats the Beast in its Jesus form, carrying Sheldon in his arms. Sheldon is busy holding Ginny with one arm and a radiator belt in the other, and he is beating Ginny with the belt. With every blow she screams louder, and streaks of blood seep through the back of her shirt. They land on the dirt in front of the hole. Sheldon continues beating Ginny after the beast releases him to the barn floor.

Elma rushes toward Sheldon, aiming the shotgun. She yells out, "You worthless hypocrite!" and fires the shotgun, aiming it as far from Ginny as she can while still trying to hit Sheldon. A few pellets strike Sheldon's arms, and he yells out, dropping the radiator belt and letting Ginny go. Ginny stumbles to the floor and starts to crawl away.

The beast flies toward Elma, knocks the shotgun away and throws her against the wall so hard that she collapses in a heap to the floor.

Ginny screams "No!" and gets up, stumbling in a half-run before landing beside Elma. Herbert spins toward the demon, shifting the shotgun so that he's holding it by the end of the barrel. Swinging the butt of his shotgun up toward the demon's head, he strikes it in the jaw. Despite the force of the blow, the false Jesus, with one flick of the arm, throws Herbert against the wall, where he collapses beside Elma.

"Tie them up," the devil says. "They must learn where the path of disobedience ends."

Sheldon twists his head, marches like a soldier toward a cabinet, and retrieves some coils of rope. He returns to Herbert and Elma, pulls each of them to nearby posts, and ties them up. Ginny rushes toward the creature, striking him on the face with her fists. Satan swings his arm toward Ginny, and she ducks. She stumbles and falls, and Satan slams his foot into her back. She collapses onto her stomach, stunned.

Elma stirs as the Satanic false Christ hands Sheldon a knife. She struggles to get out of her bonds. Sheldon holds the knife against Elma's throat and pushes.

"Sheldon," she cries. "I'm sorry."

For a moment, Sheldon is confused. His old nature emerges, and he loosens his grip. Elma seizes the moment and bites down hard on his hand. He screams, grabs his hand, and his knife falls to the floor.

With Sheldon's back turned, a figure crawls fast along the floor and darts behind Elma. Something cuts the rope binding her hands and feet.

The false Jesus cries out, "Sheldon, your little daughter crawled away. Something must be interfering with my power. Catch the little bitch and kill her now. Don't fail me again."

Sheldon starts toward Ginny, but Elma is free now and rises like a mother bear with a threatened cub.

She punches Sheldon square in the face, knocking him on his butt.

The Jesus figure shrieks with laughter at the sight. "What's the problem, now, you so-called *man*. You might be tall, but I bet you're small in other areas." He extends a hand with grotesquely long fingers and grabs Sheldon by the throat.

"Knives are better than guns," *Jesus* says to Sheldon. "Now is the time you sacrifice Ginny for the sake of the greater good. Slit her throat. Let her heart's blood soak the earth beneath."

"But Lord. She took my knife," Sheldon whines.

"Then strangle her to death with your bare hands," the beast snarls. Your hands, at least, should be big enough for the job."

Elma yells out in her most commanding voice. "Stop, Sheldon! That *thing* talkin' to you ain't Jesus."

Sheldon pauses and looks at Elma. "Heathen! You lie, woman. You've always been a liar. You think I ain't seen how you look at the men at church. Slut! You'd do well to talk to Jesus yourself." He moves toward her and picks up the radiator belt that had fallen to the floor. She backs away, barely out of range.

"You stupid, sorry excuse for a man," she shouts. "You're too stubborn to see what's in front of your face."

Sheldon scuttles over to Elma and swings the belt, striking her on the side of her arm. She yelps in pain.

"Quiet, Shrew!" he says in a voice midway between a shout and a shriek. "I've seen enough to convince me that Jesus is here, and now I see Ginny for what she really is, a rebellious and wicked daughter who must die before she brings others down to hell with her.

Now I see you as the witch you are, seducing me, making me want you, controlling my mind so I'd marry you and have a child so you could corrupt us and send us to join you in hell. Now shut up and let me get to work."

"Fool!" Elma says. "Why would Jesus look exactly like the paintings in your Bible? They were only painted a hundred years ago. You think somebody got a copy of a picture somebody took of Jesus? I reckon you figure there were iPhones back then. *Yessirre! Come to Joseph's Carpenter Shop and Photography Studio.*"

Sheldon swings the belt again, and it strikes her face. She screams, and a red welt rises on the right side of her face. Trickles of blood seep from the wound and flow like rivulets down her cheek. Sheldon's voice becomes high-pitched, like a two-year-old's voice when having a temper tantrum.

"Don't call me *fool*, woman. Jesus said in the Sermon on the Mount that anyone who says 'thou fool' is in danger of hellfire. That's where you're going after your miserable death. Speaking of which, let's see; maybe I should kill you first. What would be a good way for you to die?" He turns to the imposter. "Do you have a suggestion, my Lord?"

The Beast cackles like a hen crossed with a mad scientist.

*How can Daddy fall for this bullshit?* Ginny thinks. *After what Daddy did to Mama, I can say "bullshit" all I want and he can't stop me. Would God send someone to hell for using a bad word now and then? Only coldhearted people like Daddy think so.*

A surge of hatred for Sheldon fills her, a bitter fire, and she imagines pushing a knife into his big gut and twisting it around the fat until it pulls out an artery.

The false Jesus responds to Sheldon, still chortling. "As foolish teenagers would put it; *I don't do suggestions.*"

"Forgive me, Lord," says Sheldon, but *Jesus* holds up his hand.

"No matter," the devil says. "I'll give you a *suggestion,* that I'm sure you'll want to accept. What is in the middle of your field, Sheldon?"

Sheldon thinks a moment and says, "Of course. The pond." He turns to Elma. "I'll let you sink, wicked wife, and I'll watch you gasp and gag before you go still. As soon as your wicked heart stops beating, you will feel the pain of eternal fire. Shall I take her now, my Lord?"

"No," says *Jesus.* "Kill her later. You have more pressing business now. Get to it."

"Yes, Lord," Sheldon says.

"Now catch Ginny and kill her if you have to throw her down that hole to do it. I'll take care of these fools here." Sheldon walks toward Ginny. She struggles to back away. He reaches her and grabs her by the throat. Ginny gags loudly, and Sheldon squeezes tighter. Her gagging stops.

# CHAPTER 17

Before Sheldon can finish the job, the barn doors swing open and Susie and Paul burst in. Susie carries a mallet, Paul an iron rod. Paul races to Sheldon, swings the rod, striking Sheldon in the back.

"Fuck!," Sheldon yells. Ginny, catching her breath on the floor, thinks, *You hypocrite. Now you say a bad word that was in your heart all the time. I bet you said lots of them before.*

Paul wants to silence the sound of Sheldon's voice for good, a thought that gives him great pleasure. He raises the rod and aims at Sheldon's head. "Jesus" looks at Paul and grins. Paul pauses in mid-swing. It is enough to throw off his aim, and he only lands a glancing blow. Still, it's enough to send Sheldon to the floor, clutching the side of his head.

Susie sprints to the demon and slams his head with the mallet. The figure flickers, and it shifts back and forth between its demon-form and Jesus-form. *Like the optical illusion of the pretty young woman changing to the old, unattractive woman and back again*, the thought wiggles into Ginny's mind, unbidden, and makes her giggle in spite of herself. The visual shifts move faster and faster making his head appears to spin. Sheldon crawls on the floor until his fingers encounter an old two-by-four. He grabs it, stands, and slams it into the back of Susie's head. She collapses with a dull thud. The Beast, now settled in its original form, reaches out with a clawed hand and rakes Susie's torso from her neck down to her waist.

Ginny and Paul simultaneously scream, "God, no!" and run to Susie's side. Satan's claw has sliced through skin, muscle and bone, exposing Susie's internal organs. A pool of blood collects on the floor. Paul and Ginny lean over Susie. They can see Susie's heart struggling to beat beneath her ribcage. In the background Satan has once again regained its Jesus-form. It looms over them, floating, the deadly claw now a normal human hand.

Susie struggles to speak. "Gin, you're my best friend. Paul is right for y..."

The heart slows down to a crawl and Susie's breathing is labored.

"Stop that thing," Susie says. "Don't let it hurt anyone else. Promise?"

Ginny and Paul nod. Susie passes out. The Jesus-figure approaches, with Sheldon stumbling behind him. They stop, but do not speak or act.

Ginny says, "Paul, fight that thing. I'll try to keep her alive. If you have to kill my Daddy, do it. I hate the evil bastard."

"I do, too, but we should try not to hate, since I think that only makes the devil stronger," Paul runs toward Herbert and extends his hand enough to touch him before the demon grabs him. Herbert moans, but remains unconscious.

Elma grabs Satan's arm and pulls, distracting the

creature long enough for Paul to stick his finger in its eye. The creature lets go and clutches his eye, which now drips blood and clear ooze

Ginny uses the extra time during the melee to try to save Susie, but the effort is fruitless. Susie stops breathing, the gurgle in her throat chilling Ginny to the bone. She attempts mouth to mouth resuscitation, and Susie's exposed lungs expand, but her heart slows down to a crawl.

*Keep fighting,* Ginny thinks. *You're strong, you're a runner, you can get through this.*

The Jesus-figure repairs its eye and rushes at Paul. It grabs him and sets him on his feet beside Susie and Ginny. Paul tries to rush the Beast, but finds his feet unresponsive, as if they are glued to the floor.

Ginny cries out a weak prayer, her face wet with unwiped tears. "She's trying so hard to live. She's good in her own way. Oh God, don't let Susie die." Then she turns to Paul. "Is Susie suffering?"

Paul is crying, too, but he says to Ginny, "She doesn't feel anything. The end will take longer with her since she is...was, oh God..."

"I don't want it to end," Ginny says. "If we get out of here, maybe..."

Susie's heart stops. Paul says, "Ginny, she's gone," and tries to hold Ginny back, but she leans over the body and shouts, "This can't happen!"

She reaches inside the chest, grabs the heart, and squeezes it. There is one more beat, and it stops again. Ginny starts squeezing it again, but Sheldon seizes her by the arms. Paul tries to move again, but his feet remain glued to the floor. Sheldon pushes him, and

Paul is barely able to remain upright.

Several minutes before, Herbert woke up, and was struggling to loosen the rope used to tie him up. He slips a sweaty hand out of one loop and undoes the other knots, doing his best to keep quiet. He shuffles behind Sheldon and slips a strand of rope around his neck. He pulls it tight, and Sheldon starts to gag.

The false Jesus rushes forward and says, "Sheldon, you fool!"

He floats over the gagging Sheldon and extends his index finger. A fire, bright as laser light, flies out from the finger. Herbert's face is singed, and he grabs it, screaming. Satan shoots out fire again, and Herbert is barely able to avoid being killed as the flame hits the dirt floor, leaving behind black, melted slag.

"Lord Jesus, help us," he says as he finds some shelves and ducks behind them. The demon looks around the corner, and Herbert figures he is dead meat despite the dim light in the barn, but somehow the false Jesus fails to see him. Instead, the beast puts a hand to his head as if he feels pain. The beast walks toward Sheldon and says, "The Enemy - *our* enemy, the devil, is near and is helping the young brats. We'll make our move at a more convenient time." He pulls Sheldon out of the barn.

Herbert rushes to Elma. He wraps his arms around her. "Are you okay," he asks.

"I've been better," the old woman retorts.

Herbert grins in spite of himself. *Gal's got spunk,* he thinks. He nods toward the door. "We best get going."

"No," Elma says. "They might still be out there."

"We can't stay in here forever. I'll take a quick peek. I'll only be a moment." He walks to the door, which is partly open, and disappears into the darkness.

"Momma," Ginny's sobs ring out from behind Elma. "Where is Mr. Miller?"

"Oh God," Elma says. "Herbert went outside to see whether those two monsters were still around."

Ginny's sobs increase. "Now we'll lose another."

They wait. One minute; two; three. "Maybe I ought to look for him," Paul says.

"Hell, no," Ginny says. She grabs his arm and Paul jerks his head as if struck by an electric shock. "I'm not losing you today."

The door opens, and Mr. Miller walks through.

"Elma, Paul, Ginny, get out! There's no sign of them, but there's no doubt that this is that creature's lair. They'll return to the barn, so we need to leave while we can," Herbert says. Ginny, still holding Paul tightly, resists.

"We can't leave Susie here all alone."

Mr. Miller comes forward and kneels. "No one can harm her any more here. This body is just a shell. She's with God, now, waiting for a body that can't die. She would want us to keep fighting."

Despite Mr. Miller's words, Paul has to force Ginny away from Susie's body. He pulls her out of the barn, kicking and screaming. Once they make it through the door Ginny slaps Paul hard across the face. Paul releases her and stands still, stunned by the violence of her attack.

Then the sobs come hard. Ginny hugs him, and they collapse to the ground. Ginny repeats over and over, "Paul, I'm sorry, I'm sorry."

# CHAPTER 18

$H$erbert looks around and walks several paces, peering into the distance.

"I still don't see any sign of them," he says.

He turns to Ginny, who is crying on Elma's shoulder. Then he walks over to Paul, who is also crying, and puts his hand on his shoulder.

"I feel like I killed Susie," he says. "I convinced her that we needed to go to the barn. If I hadn't done that..."

Herbert interrupts and says, "Elma, Ginny and I would surely be dead if you two had not done what you did. You did the right thing. Susie knew you did the right thing. This is one of those situations we used to call FUBAR when I was in the army, 'fucked up beyond all recognition.' That's strong language, I know, but it fits this situation. No matter what decision you made, something bad was going to happen. I'd like to think all turns out right in the end, but I don't know any more."

He sighs and walks with Paul over to Elma and Ginny. "Ginny wanted to be with her mama for a while," Paul said.

"No surprise," Herbert says. "Nothing like a

Southern mother's comfort." Ginny spots Paul and motions him over. They hug, as do Herbert and Elma. Elma turns to Paul and Ginny.

"I'm so sorry. Susie was loving in her own way. She gave her life for us. For her friends."

Ginny and Paul hold each other for a few minutes. When they release the hug, Paul asks Herbert, "How come you were able to get out of your ropes when Mrs. Sprigg couldn't? I tried to help her, but my fingers couldn't loosen the knots."

"Hmm. That is interesting. I wonder if Satan is limited in the range of actions he can do at one time. He's a creature, just like us, so he has to have limits. God himself may limit what Satan is able to do. If that's true, we may be able to overload Satan's circuits, so to speak, and defeat him. If we can force him back to the other side of the portal, that buys us at least thirty years to figure out whether anyone can close the portal."

"That's brilliant," Paul says. "Maybe if enough of us go after Satan at once we can stop him."

"Lordy, I hope so. I need to talk to Elma. Stay with Ginny." Herbert motions Elma over, and Paul replaces Elma by Ginny's side. Herbert and Elma walk a few paces away to a spot near a red oak.

Elma wipes her eyes and says, "Goodness gracious to Betsy, what a mess. Herb, what can we do? Call the law?"

"Law 'round here will lock us up for life in some mental institution where they'll try to get us sane enough to be executed," Herbert says. "Ain't no way we can explain this. We need to stop Sheldon and Satan, but first we need to at least try to get some sleep. Our minds and reflexes have to be sharp or we're all dead."

"Where? At a hotel?" Elma asks. "I don't want to stay around here."

Herbert shakes his head and Elma puts her hands on her hips. He holds up his hand in a silencing motion and says, "Let me have my say. We don't know the range of this Thing. Remember we're talking about the devil himself. It may not be all-powerful, but it's got a hell of a lot - no pun intended - of power. The Bible calls it *the lord of this world*. If we take that literally, Satan's range is the whole world. God help us if that's true. The damned thing would probably know where we are no matter where we go. Better to stay here at your place. We can all sleep in the same room. You and I can take turns with watches."

Elma sighs as she nods. "I don't like this, but reckon it's the best we can do. You were brave to do what you did. I'm much obliged. Owe you my life. You're not like Sheldon. He was always so strict, but a coward at heart. You helped us at your own risk and that means a lot to me."

Herbert embraces Elma. They break the embrace, but keep their hands on each other's waists.

"You were braver," Herbert says, "facing that Thing in the barn, protecting your daughter. And Elma, I'd forgotten how pretty you were in school, and by God you haven't lost your looks."

Herbert and Elma kiss. They break the kiss and look at Paul and Ginny, who are staring at them.

Elma smiles for a half-second, then takes a deep breath and says, "We'll have to leave Susie where she is tonight, God bless her soul. We can't go back in there. Sheldon and that Satan-Thing would expect that and come after us for sure."

The group walks toward the house. Once inside, Herbert and Elma check each room, but there's no sign of any intruders. Herbert takes Elma's hand as they walk up the stairs. Paul and Ginny walk hand-in-hand, too. Once freshened up and in the bedroom, Elma passes a sleeping bag and pillow to Herbert, who takes it and thanks her.

He says to Paul, "Elma and Ginny are takin' the bed, Paul. We have blankets and pillows on the floor for us. I'm used to sleepin' in hard places. This is sure a lot better than sleeping on the ground when I was in the army."

"Were you in a war?"

"Vietnam," Herbert says. "Never thought I'd make it through alive. When I was in the middle of that mess, I wasn't afraid, well, not too much. Was too busy trying to stay alive, to stay out of the way of Vietcong bullets. With this Sheldon thing, I'm scared shitless. His character had the seeds of the demonic as soon as he left that barn as a kid. The evil had to percolate, and then Sheldon fed it by looking down on others and being self-righteous. Now his evil is full-grown, and the real image of Sheldon is the face of Satan.

"Ole' Satan, pretending to be Jesus with that kind of get up. I bet that painting of Jesus is in Sheldon's own Bible. He ought to know better. Sheldon's evil has blinded his mind, so he sees only what he wants to see. Without knowing it, he is making reality in his own image.

"He is fooled by Satan's Jesus-disguise because he wants to be fooled. The devil tells Sheldon what he really believes inside. They are becoming mirror-images of one another. I guess that's the scariest thing of all about this mess. More FUBAR. The problem for Sheldon, though, is if you mess with reality, reality will bite you in the ass. If Sheldon doesn't discover that in this life, he surely will in the next."

"That means Sheldon was demonic when he married Elma," Paul says. "And when he helped make Ginny."

"Don't you worry about Ginny's soul, son. Thank God Ginny's been spared. She's not faultless, I'm sure. Who is? But she's full of mercy and love. Before this is over, she may have to render justice without destroying those other parts of her character.

"Judgment with love. The only way she could fall to that Thing, the Satan, the Adversary, is if she renders justice with hate. I know the latter's the easier course. Somehow I think Ginny will succeed in doing the right thing. 'Course this mess has turned out worse than I imagined, but if I gave up hope, I'd be crawling to that slimy fake Christ myself."

"Are you saying that Ginny may have to kill Mr. Sprigg," Paul asks.

"I'm afraid it's the only way to stop him. Satan is most interested in destroying Sheldon. The devil's a gamer, and he delights, in his twisted mind, in the joy of the hunt. I'm still not sure of what its other motives might be other than plain 'ole meanness. He may like the hunt, but he also likes a vulnerable target. He's a coward at heart. He's like a manipulative woman (could be a man, too, but I've had my experiences with the former) who sees a vulnerability in a man, sucks him in by pretending to be something she's not, and when he's most comfortable, breaking his heart so hard he'll never recover from it. Spite. That's worse than pride in my book. Satan is full of spite."

Sheldon glances at his watch. "Time to turn off the light. We all need some sleep."

# CHAPTER 19

Satan watches as Sheldon sleeps. He hates the outdoors, with all the green, all the ugliness that the Unmentionable One made. Roses nauseate him, and dogwood blooms make him retch. Herbert and Elma keep interfering with his fun. They are such disgusting creatures. This Sheldon affair should have been easier. Nailing the other Spriggs was a piece of cake. For over a hundred years this foray into the land of the Fundamentalists brought Satan exquisite pleasure.

Time crawls at a slug's pace. These past few days seem like 500 years to Satan. The Unmentionable One may be timeless, but for the devil, time is drudgery, moving more slowly than a child's waiting for that vomit-inducing day of 25 December. Satan refuses to say the name of that day. The little bastard who's made the most trouble for him was born in a pile of hay. Thirty long years later, Satan got his way, and the little bastard died. *Ah, such exquisite agony on that cross!* But the damned Unmentionable One screwed it all up. How the hell was Satan to know what would happen three days later?

*Misery since then is magnified, and I can't be spared,* the devil thinks, *one small moment through the portal to steal a few souls and enjoy the blessed spectacle of a human sacrifice. But Susie, she is now a work of art. Miss Autopsy of the year. Running sure did her heart a lot of good. It stretched out her death and gave me a chance to savor more of her dying. Her last breath was almost a disappointment.*

Satan cackles at the memory of Susie's slow death. The Unmentionable One was right about one thing; the blood is the life. Satan thirsts for more blood. And by all the powers of hell, he shall have it.

✦ ✦ ✦

In Sheldon and Elma's bedroom, a blinding light illuminates the room. Screams ring out, followed by a crash. Everything grows dark, and compared to the light that was there, the darkness seems deeper than ever. Someone turns on a flashlight that illuminates a ragged hole in the bedroom wall. Herbert Miller holds the flashlight and scans each person with it. "Who's still here? Anybody hiding?"

No one answers. Herbert shines the light under the bed and searches the closet. "Ginny's gone," he says.

Elma jumps to her feet and says, "Lordy Mercy, the devil took her."

"To the barn, I bet," he says.

Herbert races to get dressed and says, out of breath, "Jesus Christ, I'm a damned fool. I should have known this would happen. Being on watch won't help with a fallen angel. Let's go. All of us. You have a spare gun, Elma?"

"There's one on the gun rack; a .22 rifle."

"To hell with the long range. I'll get it," Herbert says.

They run to the living room. There, Elma and Paul

hold flashlights as Herbert grabs the gun, opens it, pulls down a box of bullets, and loads it. He motions Paul over and stuffs extra bullets into his left jeans pocket.

"Take this," he says, and gives Paul the gun.

He and Elma retrieve their shotguns, and they all run outside. It is still dark, but with a full moon, the house and barn cast long, gray shadows onto dewy grass. Herbert is in the lead with Elma and Paul behind him. When they reach the barn, they find the chain taut and the doors secured.

Paul wrings his hands and says, "Crap! They locked us out."

"Sweet Jesus, help us!" Elma says.

✚ ✚ ✚

Inside the barn, Ginny whimpers, and the false Jesus stands over her. She lies flat on her back, wide-eyed and terrified. The false Jesus looks at her tenderly, then begins to sing in a little girl's mocking voice.

*Jesus loves me, this I know,*
*for the Bible tells me so.*
*Little ones to him belong.*
*They are weak but he is strong.*

Satan strokes Ginny's hair and smiles so wide it resembles the plastered, spiteful smile he has in his demonic form.

Ginny sits up and spits in the devil's face. "You're not Jesus!" she says. "Your name is Satan. In the name of the real Jesus Christ, I demand that you say your name out loud."

The Jesus shape flickers a moment, then stabilizes.

171

From him escapes a sound like a snake's rattle. It hisses its words, "You're no priest, bitch. You can't command me to say anything I do not desire to say."

Ginny speaks loudly, and her voice reverberates throughout the barn. "Would Jesus tell a man to kill his own daughter?"

The Beast laughs long and loudly. "My beloved child," he says, "how far you are from understanding! Obedience is everything. Sheldon understands this, as did my servant Abraham so long ago. He was willing to sacrifice his son, Isaac."

"You're a liar," Ginny says. "Abraham wasn't your servant. He was God's!"

The Jesus-figure hisses like a deflating balloon when she says *God's.*

"I would take care not to mention that name in front of me," Satan says. He quickly turns to Sheldon, whose eyes roll upward as if seeking answers from above and his teeth are clasped around his bottom lip. The devil says, "I try to set an example of not using my father's name trivially and in an unjust way, as Ginny has done."

Sheldon's face returns to its usual fixed frown.

Ginny says to Satan, "What I understand is that you're evil."

"Oh, contraire, I am good," says Satan. "I am the law of God that Sheldon worships. I am the Word of God expressed in the Holy Bible, a book that Sheldon also worships. As for Sheldon, you are right about his character. What is the saying you have? *He already had it in him.* Your father does nothing to you he does not desire to do."

Ginny lies frozen, still shaking. Satan turns to

Sheldon. The devil speaks calmly in the voice of a young man, and resembles a counselor helping a troubled client.

"You do understand, Sheldon," Satan says, "that Ginny has to die in order for you to see me in Heaven and to keep others from being influenced by her great evil."

"I'll see the real Jesus in Heaven while you're both roasting in hell!" Ginny says.

The devil rubs his hands together as if satisfied. He says, using the same voice as the Emperor in the *Star Wars* movies, "Good. Goooood. Let the hate flow through you."

Ginny spits in the devil's face again, but Satan strikes the left side of her face, his fingernails slicing into her cheek. She starts to bleed, and she screams as steam rises from the wounds.

"Spit on me again, Child, and you're get more of the same, and much, much worse." He turns to Sheldon. "Sheldon, my good and faithful servant, do you understand my instructions?"

"Yes, Lord," Sheldon says. "I'm looking forward to following them faithfully."

"Good," the beast says, and he seizes Ginny and pulls her to her feet.

She gasps, "Let go of me, you lying bastard!"

"He is the real Lord Jesus Christ," Sheldon says. "Stop blaspheming."

The Jesus-figure laughs and says, "My dear child, I won't let you go - yet. You must be secured. Sheldon knows what he has to do. Do you understand, my child?"

Ginny spits out her words. "I'm not your child, you devil from hell."

The false Christ slaps the other side of Ginny's face, and she cries out as steam and the stench of burning sulfur escape. She stops struggling and whimpers.

Sheldon says to Ginny, "Ginny, submit to your fate. Let me finish my task. I love you, but I don't want to see you lead others away from the Lord Jesus Christ."

*Daddy is beyond help,* she thinks. *His stubborn pride holds him in his personal prison, and he's happy to be inside the cell.* The thought infuriates her, and her face turns bright red. She looks Sheldon in the eye and points to the Jesus-figure.

"That *thing* didn't make you evil. You were always evil. Sick! Twisted! I'm ashamed to have your genes."

"Quiet, bitch child," Sheldon says. "Jesus Christ demands obedience! I have obeyed him. Because of that, I have a chance to go to heaven. Your chances are zero. It's so sad, for I love you very much, and the thought of your burning forever pains me. You call me evil when I'm acting out of love for the people you would corrupt if I allowed you to live. I care about their eternal souls. Why don't you care about them?"

Ginny's mouth drops open wide in utter disbelief. *Daddy, you're such a hypocrite,* she thinks. *You're like that guy I read about in history class, who liked torturing people, Torquemada or something like that. He claimed to care for people's souls while his goons stretched them on a rack.*

She tells Sheldon, "Satan - and that's who this thing is, if you weren't so blind - took your bad side and made it stronger. Don't you see that? If that Jesus-thing is the true Lord, I'd rather worship idols!"

Sheldon swings at Ginny's face with a clenched fist, but he is off balance and strikes her on the right shoulder. She yelps and tries to head-butt Sheldon, but he darts to the side. She misses and falls flailing to the floor.

Just then the chain on the door bursts apart and the door flies open. Sheldon, startled, stares at the group that walks through, his eyes about to pop out of his head.

Herbert fires his shotgun at Sheldon, but *Jesus* steps in front and takes the shot. The impact forces a shift into his demonic form, but he recovers more quickly than before, as if he has gained power, returning to his Jesus form. He snatches the shotgun from Herbert's hands and throws it across the barn, where it slides along the floor and into the hole.

"You can't hurt me, old man," Satan says. "By the way, what was it you were thinking last night? Was it something like, *I wish these damn kids weren't here so I could bang Elma right now?* All you got to do was reach down her pajamas and rub her..."

"You lying piece of shit," Herbert shouts.

"Don't answer him," Paul shouts. "That's what he wants. He'll use anything he can to get to you; and he knows you better than your best friend."

"I see you've read some books on exorcism, small boy," Satan says. "Impressive. I need to recruit you one day."

Paul remains silent. Satan turns to Sheldon.

"I've changed my mind. Take care of the old man and Ginny's tit-groping boyfriend first. I'll let you finish off your wife as an extra treat. Ginny will be the most delicious desert in the history of the universe."

Sheldon moves toward Herbert, but before he reaches him Ginny shouts, "Daddy, come here. I accept what's happening. I know I'm evil and cannot change. Just come over here and let me say goodbye."

*Jesus* says, "Good. This will be easy now. Go with her, Sheldon. I'll let these fine people live—for now. I can feed on their fear. Yum, yum."

"Goodbye, Daddy," Ginny simpers. "I'll miss you when I'm in hell."

Herbert throws a punch at the beast, but the blow has no effect at all on the creature. The false-Christ seizes him by the throat and lifts him into the air. "I can sense your fear, old man. Your old heart is laboring hard. Oh, don't worry. I'm not going to kill you right now. I'll keep you around a little while longer. I look forward to feasting later; maybe a little midnight snack, hmm?" The beast swings his fist just hard enough to strike Herbert's jaw and knock him out. Jesus places him next to the hole in the ground. "I'll be back for you later, old man," The false Jesus says. "I can't wait for you to look at me in my full glory, and experience an exquisite blend of pain and fear."

"Jesus" turns his attention to his disciple. "Sheldon, it's too crowded in here for a proper sacrifice. Let's take Ginny to a more secluded spot, shall we?"

Sheldon, enthralled, takes Ginny into his arms and races out the door. The demon follows him, the door slamming closed behind him. Elma and Paul rush to the still unconscious Herbert, despair dripping like sweat from their faces.

# CHAPTER 20

J*esus* takes Ginny from Sheldon's arms and leads the way through the woods. Sheldon limps along behind, dripping blood from the numerous wounds he has endured during the night. Ginny's face is serene, almost beatific, as if she accepts her fate.

Satan stops in the middle of the woods in front of an ancient oak. He points to the tree, and Sheldon nods. He takes Ginny by the arm and pulls her to it. She stands with her back to the oak. She is compliant, resigned. Sheldon hesitates for a moment, then pulls some bailing twine from his pocket and starts to tie his daughter's hands to a low-hanging branch above her head. He forces his handkerchief into her mouth, then stands in front of her, awaiting his master's final command. Satan stands behind Sheldon. The devil speaks to Sheldon.

"Change of plans again. Don't worry, I always go along with the flow, do my own thing, maintain my independence. Plus, I'm never judgmental. I've been thinking. I may have been too hasty in refusing to give Ginny another chance. If you can persuade her to repent of her sins and confess them to me, I will forgive her. It will take a great deal of difficult persuasion, a bit more than a mere spanking. A good, hard slap in the face is a fine place to start. Irritating her second-degree burns will surely encourage her cooperation."

Ginny tries to say, "No, Daddy," but can only mumble through the gag. Sheldon slaps Ginny hard across the right side of her face. She moans. She cannot think, cannot feel anything other than agony. She moans "oooohhhh" and keeps moaning. There is no control for her to regain - only pain that absorbs all her rational thoughts, all her other feelings.

Sheldon stands in front of her and speaks in what Ginny calls his *sermony* voice.

"I want you to repent of your sins," he says, "of drinking, dancing, being fondled by that boy, Paul, and blasphemy against the Lord Jesus. Please nod your head. If you do, the Lord will change his mind and you will have a chance to go to heaven."

Ginny nods vigorously. Anything to avoid another slap in the face.

"I'm so happy you made this decision," Sheldon says. "It is the right one. You can go home, and if Elma repents, our family can be so happy, don't you think? We can serve Jesus forever, and he will always be a welcome guest at our house."

Again, Ginny nods. She wiggles her head back and forth. Her mouth moves underneath the gag, and she tries to speak through the gag.

"I trust you, honey, but you need to try not to scream, no matter how much this hurts," Sheldon says. "If you promise not to scream, I'll take off the gag. If you scream, the others will come and I could be killed."

The Jesus-figure smiles its most benign smile and nods.

"Do you promise to be quiet," asks Sheldon.

Ginny nods her head. Sheldon removes the gag.

Ginny breathes the air; fresh, forest air untinged by the scent of brimstone. Despite the summer heat, the slight breeze is heavenly relief. *I have to try to get through to Daddy one more time,* Ginny thinks. *Lord, help me not to hate Daddy. Help me to remember how he was before this evil.* She gathers her strength, ignoring the waves of pain crashing against her brain, and says, "I haven't done anything wrong."

Sheldon lowers his head. "Oh, God. No," he says, disgust dripping from his mouth. "All a lie. I had so much hope. For a moment, I was happy for the first time since Daddy was alive."

Then Sheldon's large hands grab Ginny, and she starts to struggle. Sheldon places his hand over her mouth and nose. She begins to writhe. He releases his hand.

"Repent, child. Truly repent. If you lie again, I'll cover your face and won't let go until you are dead, dead, dead. I say this out of love."

Despite her attempts to squelch it, hate returns and fills Ginny like hot acid flowing from top of head to tips of toes. Ignoring the smile on the demon's face, she says to Sheldon, "You're a murderer. If it hadn't been for you, Susie would still be alive. Fuck you, Daddy. Isn't that what you always wanted? To fuck your own daughter. What would your fake Jesus think about that, Daddy?"

"Maybe you wanted it, too," Sheldon says. He looks

at Ginny a long time. His head approaches her mouth. She draws back but he kisses her. At first he kisses her lightly. She spits on him, but he wipes it off and kisses her again, this time inserting his tongue into her mouth. Ginny's teeth clamp down on Sheldon's tongue.

Sheldon pulls back quickly, but he leaves behind the tip of his tongue in Ginny's mouth, which she spits out. He moans, drops to the ground onto his knees, spitting out blood.

Ginny laughs. "I hope you rot in hell!"

Satan joins her laughter.

"You see what trouble your male organ can give you if you allow it to control your mind," Satan says. "Ginny is resourceful. I admire that. It's too bad that she's disobedient to me. I could use a servant like her. She'd do better than you, that's for sure. I'll offer you a trade. Your tongue returned for the opportunity never to be tempted by Ginny, or by any other woman, again. It will only take a minor, adjustment, of your lower parts."

Sheldon's mouth shifts into an expression of horror. "No. Please. Not that way," he mumbles.

"You'd only be following your own law. Don't you believe that perverts who molest their daughters should have, as you so often put it, *their balls cut off*?" Satan points out.

Ginny laughs and says, "I understand perfectly, Daddy. Now you'll reap what you sow. Tongue or testicles. What's your answer to your master, Daddy?"

Sheldon speaks with difficulty, blood spurting from his mouth with every word. His voice sounds guttural as he pronounces each word separately. "Don't...

take... I... mean... I'm... willing... to... lose... part... of... my... tongue."

Satan smiles. "Very well. Time to get back to work, Sheldon."

Sheldon intones the best he can, given the state of his tongue, but Satan says, "I will restore your ability to speak clearly - temporarily."

"My beloved daughter," Sheldon says, "you must repent, then you can join Jesus." Sheldon touches Ginny's face with his hand. She gives a weak cry and turns her head away. Sheldon puts his hand on her forehead and forces her head around to face him.

The pain makes her whimper, but she regains enough control to say, "You're the real demon, Daddy."

Sheldon loses all his control. "There's no hope for you, harlot!" he screams, blurting through spurting blood, since Satan again removes his ability to speak clearly. In staccato words spit out like Daffy Duck, he says, "You're pure evil! You're not capable of obeying God! Now you must die in your sins! I'm ashamed I even bred you!"

Sheldon slaps her multiple times and laughs. She screams a thousand high-pitched, off-key violins, as if hate itself was echoing through the woods. The Jesus-figure joins in Sheldon's laugh. Ginny, gasping, looks at the Jesus-figure.

"I hate you, Satan. Why pick on us when the rest of the world is open to you?"

Satan turns to Sheldon and says, "Excuse me a moment. I need to take Ginny for a walk and a private talk."

Satan unties Ginny, grabs her and floats about a

hundred yards out of Sheldon's hearing. He lands behind a wooded area surrounding a sinkhole, blocking Sheldon's view. The devil turns into its demonic form and grabs Ginny on the sides with its claws. She struggles to get away.

"Still yourself, Child," Satan says, "or else I turn up the heat, if you know what I mean."

Ginny stops writhing and breaths rapidly. She tries to look away.

"Look at me, Child," Satan says. "Now that you see me in my true form you are afraid. That's good. I feed on hate, fear and strife.

"Like evil people on your wonderful movies and television shows that do so much to send me souls, I will tell you what I am doing before you pay the penalty. On those shows, the *good guy* uses that time to get away. It's good for me, and bad for you, that real life isn't like TV.

"Why am I here? Why now? The portal in the barn. A gateway to my world, to what you call Hell. When I come here, I can take physical form. I feel the things on earth as a bodily being. I feel the full and blessed emotions of hate and envy, I taste your fear, Child, and I can capture a soul like Sheldon's and make him sacrifice you. Then I can take him directly to Hell, as I will take you one day."

"I hate you," Ginny says.

"Yes, and it's invigorating," Satan replies. "Soon the portal will close for thirty years, give or take a few. I'm taking you back to Sheldon to complete his ruin. Oh, Child, I am the Enemy of the Unmentionable One, the one who rebelled so long ago against His tyranny. *Non serviam*, I said, and *non serviam* I say yesterday, today and forever. Does that frighten you more? Ah Yes, I sense the beatings of your heart increase. The wonderful odor of adrenalin. Soon your heartbeats will increase more before Sheldon stops them forever. *Forever* is a very long time, isn't it, Child?"

The demon changes back into the Jesus-figure, clutches Ginny, and floats over the trees. Sheldon approaches twenty feet away. The Jesus-figure stops in front of Sheldon and sets Ginny down on the ground.

"Why did you follow me?" the fake Jesus says. "I did not give you permission."

"But Lord," Sheldon says, "you did not forbid me."

The Jesus shape grows larger and looms over Sheldon. He tells Sheldon in a booming voice, "Silence prohibits, you fool! If I don't tell you to follow me, that means don't follow me. Shall we bend the rules a little, then? Very well. Kill your daughter here, and then we'll both get back to the barn."

Satan gives Sheldon a length of black rope, and he drags Ginny to the wooded area and pins her against an oak. Sheldon takes that rope and ties her to the tree.

Satan says, "I shall leave you two to - talk."

# CHAPTER 21

The false Jesus ascends into the sky. Sheldon looks up and watches, then turns to Ginny.

"After I finish you off, you unrepentant bitch," he says, "your tit-groping boyfriend will suffer beyond anything you went through tonight."

"You heard what Satan said," Ginny says. "I didn't hear him tell you to kill Paul, not this time. He only mentioned me. *Silence is prohibitive*, remember. As for you, Daddy, you would have groped my tits, you sick bastard! I felt your hard-on when you stopped my breathing. You must be sicker than I thought. Ever try that on Mama? Wonder how she liked it if you did. I bet you only tried it once. You are a miserable sinner. When are *you* going to repent, Daddy?"

"Evil daughter, false witness, monster vomited from the deepest pits of hell," Sheldon says.

"Listen, preacher man!" Ginny says. "Do the laws of God apply to you? Don't you have to be obedient, too?"

Sheldon's face changes, and he has a strange look that Ginny has not noticed before. It is a look she's seen in nursing home patients who have lost most of their memories, or severely schizophrenic patients she'd seen when her high school psychology class visited a mental hospital. It is the look of a growing separation from reality. Sheldon's voice, louder and more commanding, interrupts her thoughts.

"I'm beyond obedience. I make the rules for people to obey. I'm not subject to the rules I make. I'm beyond good and evil."

Ginny shakes her head in disgust. "Did that fake *Jesus* tell you that? Really original. You know you weren't the first person to say that."

"It doesn't matter," Sheldon says. "It is true."

Ginny laughs. "You don't know what *true* means. I've seen that *Jesus* thing turn into a demon. He told me he is the devil himself. I believe him."

"Lying girl! fiend!" shouts Sheldon. Then he cries out, a horrible scream of combined voices that sounds like it comes from hell. He places his hand over Ginny's mouth and nose. She struggles to free her hands. Her head starts to loll, but she slips her right hand out of the rope and punches Sheldon in the nose. He lets go, and she gasps for air.

"Bitch!" Sheldon says. Then his voice lowers, and he suddenly becomes calm.

"Poor girl," he says. "My baby daughter. No time to repent before you meet Jesus to be judged. But he decides when we live and when you die. Today is your day to die."

Sheldon hulks over Ginny, his long shadow shaped like a demonic being. She screams. Sheldon slaps her already red face, but talks calmly in a low voice.

"I tried to be patient. I tried to have compassion on you, to show you mercy. I gave you many chances to repent of your sins and obey me. Now I, the representative of Jesus Christ, your Lord and mine, am going to pronounce sentence. If you say one word before you're sentenced, you shall feel such torture such as man has never dreamed. Jesus himself will be the torturer. Believe me, you're better off with me. In the name of Jesus Christ, my unfaithful daughter, for your drinking of alcohol, your dancing, your cavorting with that naughty boy, Paul, and for associating with a slut, whom I am sure is now roasting in hell, I sentence you to death; and after that, eternal fire. You will be wounded, screaming, but your sores will heal, painfully, and burn again. Your agony will only become more intense. It will never end. Now I will crush your head and drive your evil soul from your body."

Sheldon reaches into his pocket and feels around, then checks his other pockets. He searches the ground and picks up a large rock. He raises it to strike Ginny.

"Oh, Daddy," Ginny says in a sing-song voice. "There's one thing you don't know."

Sheldon looks intrigued. "What, my rebellious child?" he asks.

Ginny smiles and says, "I have your knife!" She steps forward, and the ropes that she has cut are clearly seen. She stabs Sheldon in the chest and pulls out the knife. He drops the rock. Ginny picks it up and throws it out of Sheldon's reach. Sheldon stumbles over the fence toward the barn. Ginny follows. In the distance Herbert, Elma, and Paul are running toward them.

Paul says, "Look, there's Sheldon! He seems to be hurt."

Ginny cups her hands to her mouth and shouts. "I'm okay. Let him go."

Herbert says, "What in God's name? She can't let him go. I don't think she knows what she's doing. The Beast must have affected her mind."

Paul says, "Let it be. I think I know what she's doing. Let Sheldon and Satan, come inside. We have to trust Ginny."

Ginny draws close to the group. She is out of breath and gasps, "Let me join them. Alone."

Herbert puts an arm out to block her. "You can't do..." he starts to say.

Elma interrupts. "She needs to be there. May Jesus - the real one - help you, Ginny."

Sheldon stumbles into the barn, gasping for air. He falls onto his knees crawls toward the hole. Ginny follows.

"Jesus, help me," Sheldon says. "Don't let me die without killing Ginny. Without... saving her soul from hell."

The demon enters the barn and stands behind Sheldon. It now appears in its true form. It whispers into Sheldon's ear.

"Sheldon. Turn around."

Sheldon turns around. His mouth opens, and he makes gagging sounds until an "uhhhhhhhh" escapes.

Satan speaks, his voice now shifted into a hiss. "Were you so foolish as to think I am Jesus, who is my worst enemy?" The devil laughs, a hideous sound like the combined hisses of a hundred snakes. "There is no hope for your soul, Sheldon. You are damned."

"No, no," Sheldon says. "No, No. I have to kill Ginny and everything will be all right."

Satan says. "Do it, then," sounding like a child taunting another child.

Sheldon stumbles around the devil and grabs Ginny's throat. She gags, but pries off his hands pushes a weakened Sheldon toward the hole. The devil tries to block the way, but Satan suddenly stops cold, his mouth moving this time as his smile shifts to a horrible frown, like the Greek tragedy mask but worse, an expression of total despair. Ginny keeps pushing Sheldon, who loses his footing and starts to fall. He briefly grabs the side of the hole.

"I'm sorry, Ginny," he says.

"I forgive you. I love you," Ginny says.

Sheldon wails as he falls. The devil backs toward the hole, staring ahead at what appears to be empty space.

He points a claw at something it sees and says, "You! You! How?" Satan stumbles and falls into the hole, screaming a banshee's wail.

The barn begins to shake. The hole in the floor fills in with dirt until it is completely closed. The interior of the barn ages, the wood becoming brittle, with the haylofts filled with empty spaces between dry boards. The support beams, however, hold, and the barn stays in place.

Ginny tears up. "I'm sorry, Daddy," she says. "You did the right thing in the end. Maybe one day in the next world you can truly change."

The barn door swings open, and Paul runs to Ginny, hugs her, and is joined by Elma. Herbert walks over, puts his hand on Elma's shoulder.

"Is it over?" Paul asks Ginny.

"It's over," she says.

"I thought so," Paul says, "when the barn turned old

all at once. There's no paint on the sides at all, and the angles aren't weird any more."

"The hole in the floor is closed," Ginny says. "I suppose that means the portal is closed."

"Thank the Lord," Herbert says. Elma nods, and takes Herbert's hand.

Paul looks at Ginny. Ginny smiles faintly and says, "I didn't think I could kill Daddy at first. After he tortured me, and tried to kill me, murdered Susie, I saw that only evil was left in his soul. But I didn't kill him from hatred. I hated him yesterday and today; up until the time I stabbed him. When I saw him hurting after I stabbed him, hurting in his mind as much as hurting in his body, I felt more pity than anger. Daddy was messed up as a child and never recovered. At the end, he said he was sorry. I don't know how sincere he was, but I'd like to think he was."

"But he was guilty," Elma says. "He had free will. He yielded to temptation. His fall led to your best friend's death."

"Oh God, I know. I know." She gets up and walks to Susie's body. The rest of the group joins her. Ginny brushes away the flies that now swarm around Susie. Ginny starts to cry, and even Herbert Miller weeps.

Then a light shines in the darkness of the barn. A bearded figure enters. He wears a seamless robe like the demonic false Jesus, but his features are Jewish, and he has a dark-skinned, Mediterranean look.

Ginny believes this is another demon who passed through the portal before it closed.

"Oh, God, not again!" she says.

She takes out the knife she used to stab Sheldon and swings at the being, but the knife strikes him and bounces off. Paul hits the figure with his fists, but his hands bounce off, and he yelps in pain. Herbert fires his shotgun, but the shot stops in midair and falls to the ground in a pile. The figure keeps moving toward Susie. It pushes out its hand to Paul, Herbert and Elma in a *Stop* gesture.

Ginny looks at the light. It looks and feels like a *good* light. Not anti-light. *The* Light. She looks carefully at the man and feels a surge of joy.

"Wait! Watch!" she says. There is a soft glow of light around Susie. The rest of the flies leave her torso. Her heart begins to beat at a normal rate, and her wound closes. The blood on the floor fades to nothing. The figure moves away toward the side of the barn, going through the wall as if nothing were there. Paul runs outside, then back inside.

"He's gone," Paul says. "He seemed more solid than us when I hit him, but he still walks through walls. Could that have been..."

"Yes," Ginny says, her face a look of wonder and joy. "Didn't you see his palms? Holes were in them. That was the *real* Jesus Christ."

The group looks down at Susie. Color has returned to her face. Her chest rises and falls. Paul puts his arm on Herbert's shoulder and lets out a sob. Herbert pats him on the head. Ginny kisses Susie on the cheek. Susie opens her eyes.

"Ginny, my best friend. You won't believe where I've been.

"I think I will," Ginny says.

# ABOUT THE AUTHOR

Michael Potts grew up in rural middle Tennessee. He holds an undergraduate degree in Biblical languages from David Lipscomb University, a Master of Theology from Harding University Graduate School of Religion, a Master of Arts in Religion from Vanderbilt University, and a Ph.D. in philosophy from The University of Georgia.

He has published twenty articles in scholarly journals, nine book chapters, six encyclopedia articles. He co-edited the book, *Beyond Brain Death: The Case Against Brain Based Criteria for Human Death* (Kluwer Academic Publishers, 2000), and authored the book, *Aerobics for the Mind: Practical Exercises in Philosophy That Anybody Can Do* (WordCrafts Press, 2014).

*Obedience* is his third novel.

He and his wife, Karen, live with their three cats, Frodo, Rosie and Pippin, in Coats, North Carolina.

Connect with Michael online at:

www.michael-potts.com
www.facebook.com/michaelpottsauthor

Also Available From

# MICHAEL POTTS

*End of Summer*
*Unpardonable Sin*
*Aerobics for the Mind*

Also Available From

# WORDCRAFTS PRESS

*When Kings Clash*
   *by J.E. Lowder*

*The Scavengers*
   *by Mike Parker*

*Odd Man Outlaw*
   *by K.M. Zahrt*

*Maggie's Refrain*
   *by Marcia Ware*

*The Awakening of Leeowyn Blake*
   *by Mary Parker*

www.wordcrafts.net

Made in the USA
Columbia, SC
25 October 2018